Danger Crossed

Moments

Table of Contents

Killer at the Door   Jackson/8
Scene of the Crime   Britton/20
The Drifter   Jackson/31
Mirror Image   Britton/38
Date with a Stranger   Jackson/48
Redemption   Britton/55
Responsibility   Jackson/61
The Secret Admirer   Britton/71
The Muse Incarnate   Britton/84
Girls who Lie Down with Wolves   Britton/103
Kinfolk   Britton/120
Run if you Can   Jackson/125

About the Authors   147

Danger Crossed Moments
An Anthology
By
Vickie Britton and Loretta Jackson

Treble Heart Books
1284 Overlook Dr.
Sierra Vista, AZ 85635-5512
http://www.trebleheartbooks.com

The characters and events in this book are fictional, and any resemblance to persons, whether living or dead, is strictly coincidental.

ISBN: 1-931742-22-7

Review

Danger-Crossed Moments is a macabre collection of eleven short stories, each with either a touch of the supernatural, or murder and mayhem.

Vickie Britton and Loretta Jackson, sisters who co-author, have put together an awesome collection of short stories. While reading, I felt as if I were being held in a mind puzzle. Is it him? Is it her? Who the heck do you believe? I wanted to yell, "No! Don't trust him!" or "Run! He's the murderer!" I never knew who was going to turn out to be the killer.

All the short stories are cleverly written by this duo. My only complaint is that I didn't want them to end!

Stacey Bucholz

—ALLABOUTMURDER Reviews

Acknowledgements

Date with a Stranger; Writer's Journal,1990; The Drifter, Wellspring, 1992; Responsibility, Creative Reading, 1992; Redemption, 3rd place winner, Garden State Horror Writer's Contest, 2000.

Thanks to Susan Bodendorfer, who first published the following stories as Wordbeamette singles: Girls who Lie Down with the Wolves, Kinfolk,Mirror Image, Redemption and The Muse Incarnate. With special thanks to our editor, Jeanine Berry, and to Pat Rasey, Sue Hartigan, and all our friends at allaboutmurder.com

Special Acknowledgement: Treble Heart Books would like to thank and acknowledge Mr. Terrance Agnew, model for the Danger-Crossed Moments book cover.

Introduction

In every person's life there comes a crucial moment where time is of the essence, where the clock is ticking, and a split-second decision can mean the difference between win or lose, revenge or forgiveness, or even life or death. These moments can be psychological or they can be a physical danger.

As sisters and co-authors of over thirty suspense novels the two of us are used to dealing with the concept of danger. Sometimes we get our inspiration from the world's best teacher…life.

"My first danger-crossed moment came when I was a teenager," Vickie says. "I decided to hitch a ride home from school. I jumped into a battered old truck, not yet noticing the man's gold teeth or the most evil-looking smile I had ever seen. The minute he started driving, he began talking crazy. He wouldn't stop the truck when I asked him to. At the last stop light in town I made a leap for the door and jumped out. To this day, I believe this split-second decision may have saved my life."

This frightening experience inspired two stories, "The Secret Admirer" and "Girls Who Lie Down With Wolves," both about young women, one who copes with fear of a stranger, a stalker; the other with fear of a lover who grows increasingly dangerous in his unrelenting obsession.

"I experienced a true-life danger-crossed moment," Loretta recounts, "when in the middle of the night I was awakened by a frantic pounding on the door. I looked out to see a man, a total stranger, covered with blood. Where had he come from? Was this a ploy to get admitted to the house so he could rob and kill? Not knowing what to do, I took a chance and opened the door. The stranger turned out to be a victim who, after being beaten and robbed, had been dumped off at the side of the road. The police were called, and he was taken away by ambulance to the hospital where he survived serious injuries. But the haunting memory remained with me, surfacing in the story "Killer at the Door."

These harrowing experiences caused us to take a closer look at how much a single moment might affect a person's entire life. So we challenged each other to come up with one situation after the other, each more dangerous than the last. The result is the creation of this anthology about characters at a crossroad, ready to throw caution to the winds. Some might make the right decision, others the wrong one. But all will make a choice that will affect the rest of their lives. We hope you will enjoy these stories and, while you read them, remember your own Danger Crossed Moments.

Killer at the Door
By Loretta Jackson

Doris must make a life-or-death decision when a blood-splattered stranger pounds on the door of her isolated cabin. Is he a desperate victim or a deranged killer?

Doris, irritated by a knock on the door, remained at the typewriter to finish her sentence. She hadn't expected or wanted anyone to disturb her. That's why she had rented this isolated cabin fifteen miles from the small town of Manning. The cabin was located on a lonely road where few passed and nobody lingered.

She had left Sioux Falls three weeks ago, right after the funeral, car filled with stacks and stacks of her husband's notes. It seemed natural that she would return to the district Jim and she knew best, on the edge of the Pine Ridge Reservation. Jim's work had started here; here she would find the solitude it would take to finish it. She would herself complete his book, the culmination of his vast and brilliant study of Native American culture, a work that would keep him alive. Doris, alone, understood his message well enough to give his book real form and meaning. She knew she must publish it at once while the memory of the young professor still glowed brightly in the minds of his colleagues.

The knock became louder, a pounding. Total return to reality brought with it the familiar headache, the stiffness caused from long hours at the typewriter. Probably a stranded motorist wanting to use the phone, she thought.

Almost midnight—she wasn't surprised; often she lost track of time. She switched on the porch light and lifted the heavy gray drape from the glass panel.

Eyes, close to the glass, frantic, glazed, bored into hers. Blood, all over him, sprang from a deep, jagged gash on his head. Blood flowed into the sandy hair, drenched the white shirt. He raised a large, imploring hand, leaving splotches of blood on the pane.

"My God!"

Doris snatched her fingers from the night latch she had been about to open and shrank back toward the phone. The sheriff from Manning could be here in fifteen or twenty minutes. Since she had arrived, no one had called her, nor had she made any calls. The receiver tight against her ear sounded dead. Had the phone ever worked? She tried again and again to get a dial tone, but heard only the same stillness that engulfed the room.

The pounding started again. The erratic banging of fists frightened her more than the silent phone.

Doris approached cautiously and looked out again.

"You must..." he gasped, "you must help me!"

Even since her last glimpse of him, he had grown weaker. What if he died and she had not even tried to assist him? No matter how she felt about it, no matter how frightened she was, she must open the door. She had to admit him, attempt to stop the flow of blood that if not quelled soon would surely kill him.

Doris unlocked the latch and reached out to assist him. Just inside the doorway, he staggered and despite her frenzied efforts to catch him, fell. She stared at the wide shoulders, the thick hair, tawny in the direct light, at the blood soaking into the carpet. As she turned him around, his eyes opened, light eyes, a blue-gray. She watched them fill with pain, flicker, close. He attempted to speak, but his words were muffled, incoherent. He kept repeating what sounded like the same warning over and over. Doris bent closer, straining to obtain some meaning. "You must...lock...lock the door!"

With stiff, nervous motions, she whirled, slammed the door shut and clicked the lock. Turning back to him, she spoke with voice as muffled as his. "Who's out there?"

His answer was impossible to comprehend. Plaintively, like a child, he stretched out his hand to her. The effort seemed to exhaust him. As his arm dropped, his eyes fell shut.

Doris headed to the bathroom to get a towel. Carefully she washed blood from his face, a broad face that probably always had upon it the outline of a beard.

The cold water momentarily revived him. "I stopped to change a tire." Ragged intakes of breath cut into his words. "When he stopped, I thought he was going to help me. He hit me with the tire iron." A gurgling sounded deep in his throat. "My wife started screaming. He struck her down right in front of me. He killed her."

"She's dead? Are you sure?"

His moan and the word, "Yes," ran together.

"How did you get away?" Doris gave him no time to answer. "Did he follow you?"

"I'm on foot. This is the only house anywhere around. He knows that. He has to kill me." His voice shook with pain. "I can identify..."

"You had better not try to talk."

"Janet's dead!" His hands, clutching her, possessed overwhelming strength. He clung to her, desperate sobs racking his body.

"No matter what's happened," she said, "you must be strong. Janet would expect that of you." She continued talking to him softly, her words comforting, but untrue, the way she had talked to Jim. After a while his raspy breathing began to grow calmer, more rhythmic. She eased him back against the carpet, wiping at damp blood on her blouse.

His eyes opened again, helpless, entreating. "Do you have a gun?"

Jim and she had spent many an afternoon at target practice competing for first place. She had become as good a shot as he, and she had stuffed the revolver that they shared into her suitcase before leaving the university. Obediently, she went into the bedroom and with trembling hands placed shells into the cylinder before returning to the front room.

Had his breathing become dangerously faint? She knelt beside him, listening. His breath was barely audible, but steady. Doris laid down the gun and searched his clothing for some clue to who he was. Her fingers shook as she opened his billfold—a picture of a pretty, dark-haired woman, lots of cash, a South Dakota driver's license: Gordon Litel, born 1959, Mission, South Dakota. She didn't know much more about him than she had before, except that the picture of the sweet-faced wife made her hear the screams and envision the brutal blows.

A sharp rapping sounded at the door. The gun felt icy as she gripped it, rising. She could sense the presence of the person who stood on the other side. She felt her heart begin to beat irregularly and the strength drained from her legs. "Who's there? Who are you?"

"You must let me in!"

Doris raised the drape and let it fall back in place. In this instant of vision she glimpsed strong, well-defined features. Sensitive dark eyes, the tense way his lips compressed, made her think of Jim. Jim's face began merging with his, began urging her to throw open the door and be safely enfolded in strong arms.

Doris backed away. She could no longer trust her own eyes. Had she become that frightened—beyond reality or logic? She must not allow herself to give into panic.

"I know he's in there! There's blood all over the porch."

"There's no one here."

She had expected to encounter someone drunk or crazy. Why did he sound so controlled, so sensible? "I know you're afraid. But you mustn't be afraid of me. I came here to help you."

Doris decided to take another quick look. He stood tall, lean, very straight. She could see that he was struggling to conquer some emotion. Was it fear? Rage? If only she could read the truth that carved sharp lines between brilliant, dark eyes.

The curtain fell. Was he an Indian? ...enough Indian blood, she supposed, to make his coal black hair, long enough to stir with the wind, limp and straight. "Who are you?"

"Arlin Tutt. I've been driving all day to get to Pine Ridge."

"Why did you follow him here? How did he get hurt?"

"They had stopped at the roadside park. His wife and he must have been fighting, and she struck him with a tire iron. He evidently lost control. When I drove up, he was still beating her. She was dead!" He paused, sucking in his breath. "He ran when he saw me. I knew he couldn't get far."

Doris glanced back at the man on the floor. What was she going to do? She felt blood drain from her face, a face that must be as ghastly white as his.

"Let me in!"

The silence hung fearfully around her.

"I'm trying to save your life. He has nothing to lose. He will kill you." As he spoke, the door handle turned and the wood creaked a little as if a strong shoulder were being pressed against it. "You must let me help you!"

If you want to help," Doris said, "go to Manning and get the sheriff." She waited, scarcely breathing. She was certain he hadn't left. She visualized his agile form, so very straight, waiting, maybe retreating a little back into the shadows not penetrated by the porch light.

"Are you still there?"

"If I leave, you won't be alive when I get back."

Doris's eyes darted again at the man named Gordon. He hadn't so much as moved in a long time. If he hadn't looked so very helpless, she might have wavered. She might, gun in hand, have taken a chance and opened the door. "He is...in very bad shape. I'll be all right."

"You won't be all right!" Why did he have to sound so much like Jim, exasperation mixed with responsibility. "I can't just leave you."

This time the quietness lasted much longer. It gave her time to think. Arlin Tutt, if that was his name, would have little trouble breaking into the house. No doubt that's what he intended to do. Her hand tightened on the gun. Shooting at bottles and black circles on paper was a much different thing than shooting at flesh and blood. If he decided to break in, would she even be able to shoot him?

"Don't you understand, this man is dangerous! Your life depends on me. Now, unlock the door."

"Manning is the closest town. Fifteen miles west. It's not on the reservation. The sheriff's office is just inside the city limits." Once more, unable to move or breathe, she waited.

"I'm going to break the lock!"

Her heart sank as he affirmed her greatest fear. She knew he had stepped back so he could throw his weight against the door. She knew the lock would not withstand his strength.

"If you do," she said quietly, "I'll shoot you."

"You're not going to shoot anyone." His voice was calm with certainty.

Doris raised the gun, aimed it toward the corner of the room and pulled the trigger. The bullet zinged loudly, leaving a small, neat hole in the wooden paneling. Her action must have been a correct one, must have brought the point home, for she thought she heard departing footsteps.

What was he going to do now? Certainly he had no intention of going to Manning after the sheriff.

"We've got to get out of here," she said. When Gordon didn't respond, she mopped the wet towel again and again across his face. At last his eyes opened. Recognition slowly dawned, and he tried without success to speak.

"You must get up. I'll help you."

As they struggled, Doris continued talking, her voice just above a whisper. "My car is in the adjoining garage. It's the only chance we have."

Inch by inch they crossed the front room. She laid the gun down so she could use both hands to hold him. He had unimaginable weight. At the two small steps leading to the cement floor of the garage, he swayed precariously.

Doris, carefully balancing her weight against his, edged around in front of him in time to prevent his falling. "You must step down. Lean on me. We're almost there."

She panted for breath and cold sweat covered her by the time she got him safely into the car. Once under the wheel she remembered that she had left the gun on the kitchen counter. She fled back into the house and returning, placed the revolver close beside her on the seat.

She wouldn't risk opening the garage door. The thin plywood was badly deteriorated. It would offer little resistance. She started the car, stepped down hard on the gas pedal. Wood ripped, tossed here and there by the ramming vehicle.

As they tore away from the garage, she saw a tall, lean figure illuminated by the porch light. His form, rigid, poised, loomed only a few feet from where he had talked to her. She had been right. He had had no intention of leaving.

In the frenzy of their departure, she got only a quick impression of his car—that it was blue or black, that it was a late-model. But she would never, even if they did make it to Manning, be able to describe it to the sheriff.

Fields, bare, deserted, swept past them. The blacktop road, narrow and winding, was not intended for speed. She must drive skillfully, carefully. She had often heard of the tragic wrecks caused by fast-moving cars suddenly careening on to the soft shoulders.

"Where are we going?" Gordon Litel's voice was faint, but decipherable.

"I must get you to a hospital. There's a small one in Manning."

She could barely make out his muttered protest, "I don't want to go there."

Doris glanced quickly at him. His eyes, glazed, illogical, imprinted themselves in her mind as she turned again to watch the road. Her heart sank. This man could easily be a murderer. If he were, like a crazed animal caught in a trap, he would freely strike out to protect himself and his crime. The thought that she might have made the wrong decision turned her blood to ice. She forced herself to say, "I'll notify the authorities. They'll protect you. You'll be safe once we get to Manning."

"A sitting duck," he said.

"You've lost too much blood already. There's nothing else we can do."

She did not look at him, but she could feel his burning eyes staring at her. They seemed irrational and so very fierce.

"No!" His voice sounded louder, stronger. "Keep driving! Take me to Rapid City."

"I can't do it. It's way too far." Doris glanced in the rearview mirror, her eyes fastening on the distant headlights. If only she knew which one of them to believe. For an instant, no doubt because he reminded her of Jim, she wanted Arlin Tutt to catch up with them, to perform some miracle, as John Wayne did in the old movies she watched.

But she wasn't sure which one of them had told her the truth. She stepped down harder on the gas. The man who relentlessly pursued them must have a motive to do so. He would not, she told herself emphatically, be willing to endanger his own life in order to save her, a stranger.

Doris rolled down the window a little. Sharp, cold air blew against her face. Jim had died on a night exactly like this—dark, moonless. Doris remembered the way she had felt on the way to emergency—the queasiness, the ineffective things she had said and done, the frustration, angry, powerless: Jim was dying and she couldn't prevent it.

Gordon was looking more alert. He now spoke harshly. "Don't stop at Manning."

"I am going to do what I think is best."

They both reached for the gun between them at the same time. His quickness surprised her. With the revolver in his hand, he slid over against the door.

The nagging qualms that had been warning her of his guilt now changed to full realization. He wouldn't have taken up the gun unless he intended to use it.

"You don't have to worry about your safety. I intend to pull in directly to the sheriff's office."

"We'll never get inside."

"Does he have a gun?"

"No doubt."

"I don't have gas enough to get to Rapid City." Doris's gaze fell to the gauge. Why hadn't she filled up with gas when she had gone to Winthrop for groceries? The black line was almost directly on empty. "We might not even get to Manning."

The station at the crossroads where she usually bought gas was just ahead. She peered anxiously toward the dark outline of buildings, the station, the grass-covered sunshade supported by long poles, the cabin in back, where Standing Elk, an old man who moved very slowly, would be asleep.

Standing Elk was her only neighbor. But pulling to a stop

here would solve nothing. If she did manage to rouse Standing Elk, he would be murdered, too. She couldn't take the risk.

Making a decision to go on, Doris drove even faster. In spite of her speed, the headlights behind her kept getting closer.

She tried to shut them out, to shut Gordon out. She concentrated on the road. Isolated fields rushed by so fast she felt dizzy.

Her heart seemed to stop in her chest when it first happened, the small hesitation as she pressed the gas pedal. The hesitations kept getting more and more frequent, until the car began to make protesting noises like quick and sudden coughs.

Doris felt the car losing speed. They couldn't run out of gas. Not now. Not when the headlights were so very close behind.

She had made a mistake not trying to rouse Standing Elk. The car was slowing, was stopping. Doris could do nothing but steer it to the side of the road.

"What are you doing?" Gordon was pointing the gun at her. "You can't stop here!"

"We're out of gas."

Doris skimmed the lonely fields for help. She felt an urge to jump from the car and run, but there were no trees, no protective shelter. Nowhere near were any signs of aid—just emptiness, isolation.

In the gleam of dashboard light she watched the change that came over Gordon. He no longer looked helpless, but threatening, like a raging bear that stands, prepared for a fight to the death.

The car behind them skidded to a stop. A dark form leapt out. Doris held her breath as the shadow swiftly approached Gordon's side of the car.

Gordon, steadying the gun with both hands, leveled it. As he did, the dash light illuminated his features. They were set in fury. This was exactly the way, she thought suddenly, that he had looked when he had struck and killed his wife.

Doris's head spun. She glimpsed Arlin Tutt's face through the window, a face that looked so much like Jim's.

She didn't know whether he had a weapon or not. She must help one or the other and her decision meant life or death. It must be right! She drew in her breath, then lunged toward Gordon, grabbing frantically for the gun.

In the struggle the barrel was forced upright. The sharp zap of a bullet penetrated the edge of the glass.

In a blur of motion she could see Arlin reaching inside, his strong fingers locking around both of Gordon's wrists. Giving them a powerful wrench, he shouted, "Take the gun from him!"

The revolver slipped easily into her hand.

"Give the gun to me," Arlin said.

"Don't!" Gordon cried.

Doris looked from one to the other, then she handed the gun to Arlin.

"Why don't you get in the back seat of my car," Arlin said to her. He half-dragged Gordon from her vehicle to the front seat of his own car. Once behind the wheel, he swung toward her.

Once more, as he lifted the revolver, uncertainty gripped her.

"Take this," Arlin said, handing her the gun. "Keep it aimed directly at him until we get to Manning."

The silence of the high-speed drive was broken only by the harsh sounds of Gordon's sobbing.

Doris could not bear to look down at Gordon as the men lugging the stretcher took him away.

The sheriff first spoke privately with Arlin, then wanted a statement from her.

When she left the hot, cluttered office, she found Arlin waiting. Dark eyes, sensitive, like Jim's, watched her as she crossed the room. A trace of a smile appeared in their depths.

Gratitude and relief flooded over her. She had come so close to making a wrong choice. "I should have believed you all along," she said. "But I really didn't think anyone would do what you did. You so willingly put your own life in danger to save a total stranger."

"Why not?" Arlin asked. The trace of a smile changed to one real and genuine. "Didn't you do exactly the same thing?"

Scene of the Crime
By Vickie Britton

When Sheryl returns to her high school reunion to settle an old score, she finds she's not the only one out for revenge.

Sheryl had once daydreamed of appearing at her high school reunion Hollywood-style, chauffeured in a limousine, wearing some dazzling Paris creation.

The week before the reunion, she got a haircut. It was an act of petty rebellion; Ross had always liked it long. The ill-fated haircut seemed to start a domino reaction of unpleasant events that ended in Ross leaving her.

And so it was that Sheryl pulled up in the parking lot of Escalante High in her battered Chevy, alone, armed against her private ghosts with only a purse full of cigarettes—and a handgun.

Of course, the haircut was only a link in long chain of disagreements between them. The real reason Ross left was because of Corry. Corry, with his ice-blue eyes and Polo shirts; Corry, whose image still lurked in that frightened place in Sheryl's mind where the past bears just as much importance as the future. Once again, Corry had risen up like a ghost from the grave to destroy her happiness. Now, more than ever, she realized that what he had done to her had blighted her entire life.

Sheryl didn't know exactly when the idea of vengeance began to take form in her mind. Maybe it was the moment she discovered Ross's gun was still in the glove compartment of her car. At the last rest stop the gun, which Ross always kept loaded, somehow worked its way from the glove box into her purse.

Now, Sheryl felt unexplainably guilty, as if she were the criminal returning to the scene of that secret, unexposed crime. She tried to still the violent pounding of her heart. She had nothing to fear. Her crime was yet to be committed, the murder weapon as safely concealed in her purse as if it lay at the bottom of the sea. At this moment, she was still the victim.

Damp beads of sweat formed upon Sheryl's brow. Her reluctant eyes trailed beyond the stone school building to the rectangular oval of the football stadium, then to the dark path just beyond. Time and distance had dulled the memory, but now it surfaced, as ugly and impossible to ignore as a long-dead corpse washed up on a public beach. It was there ten years ago, in that dark cluster of bushes, that Corry Hall had raped her.

As Sheryl approached the reception table, she felt herself growing unaccountably smaller. The new haircut made her self-conscious. Ross had been right; it made the large, port-wine birthmark that stained the left side of her face even more noticeable.

Sheryl's footsteps slowed. She despised the way coming back here made her feel. There was a moment when she might have abandoned her plans, turned around and walked back out the door. But now it was too late. She had been recognized. She felt Patti's eyes drift toward the birthmark and fasten there like a magnet. "Why, it's Sheryl! Sheryl Lanek!"

Sheryl faced the women who formed the Escalante

Welcoming Committee. Patti, Cynthia, and Marge. She remembered all three of them—mostly in terms of humiliations. The Broken Mirror Incident, the Ugly Picture Incident.

Sheryl was surprised to find that she held no particular resentment toward them now, only a slight annoyance as if they were flies buzzing around the dinner table. She felt the weight of the gun in her handbag. The score she intended to settle was with Corry alone.

"So tell us," Patti insisted as she handed her a program and name tag. "What have you been doing since graduation? Are you working?"

Patti Wagner looked almost the same as when her locker had been down the hallway from Sheryl's. The same smooth skin and wavy brown hair, the same saccharine smile. As if hypnotized, Patti's curious brown eyes kept slipping back to the birthmark.

Through the years, Sheryl had grown accustomed to the whispered comments, the often rude stares at the left side of her face. Though sometimes it hurt to see an occasional man's smile disappear at the turn of her head, or to catch a stranger's eyes glancing quickly away, she had stopped thinking about surgery, stopped trying to hide the discolored skin with thick makeup. She had learned to accept the mark as a unique, undeniable part of herself.

Of course, in school, it had been different. In school, she might as well have borne the mark of Cain. Ants and spiders crawled inside of her new Halston blouse. In Patti's eyes she was still "poor Sheryl." She knew now that no Paris clothing, no fine limousine, would ever have changed that. She raised her eyes to Patti's and fought the urge to run. "I'm between jobs right now."

"Well, then, are you married?" Patti persisted.

How could they be doing this to her after all these years? She felt the sense of failure being driven home as surely as a stake through her heart. "I'm currently...separated."

Sheryl was spared from more painful interrogation by a

sudden voice at her side. "Well, aren't we all? Divorced or separated, I mean." The platinum-haired woman who moved up beside Sheryl emphasized her words with a cynical, arched brow. "I don't suppose you remember me, Sheryl. I'm Dawn. Dawn Jordan."

"Of course." Sheryl smiled over the disapproving faces of the welcoming committee. The introduction had been unnecessary, despite an obvious change in hair color. Pretty Dawn Jordan had once been the talk of Escalante high.

Dawn's eyes fluttered rainbow-colored shadow at her. "God, it seems like such a long time ago we skipped gym class together, doesn't it?"

"Another lifetime," Sheryl agreed.

"Even before Divorce Number One." Dawn rested a light finger on Sheryl's arm. "Come have a drink with me, and we'll exchange sad stories." Relieved, Sheryl followed her from the reception desk, toward the bar in the corner of the decorated gymnasium.

"See anyone you know?" Dawn whispered as they moved across the tackily decorated gym, searching converted cafeteria tables in the darkness for familiar faces. Sheryl recognized few people. Only the-most-likely-to's usually bothered coming back for the reunions.

"Purple streamers—yuk—reminds me of prom night. I hate reunions. Don't know why I bothered to come," Dawn said.

Sheryl searched the darkness for people she knew. Once, Sheryl's breath caught in her throat at the flash of short, pale golden hair. She exhaled carefully. Not Corry. Only a stranger.

"I thought maybe I'd see one of my old flames here tonight," Dawn confessed as they moved up to the bar. "Maybe Rudy or Winston or someone will be here. Or that football player we all used to be so crazy about. Remember Corry? Corry Hall?"

"Yes, Corry." The sudden mention of his name made her voice slightly choked. "Do you think he'll be here tonight?"

Dawn slowed to study Sheryl carefully. "You aren't still carrying a torch for him, are you?"

"Something like that."

Dawn's laughter was like the tinkle of harsh music. "He'll be here."

"How can you be sure?" Ice formed around Sheryl's heart. A part of her began to hope that he wouldn't show.

"Isn't it the winners like him the rest of us losers come to see?" Dawn's next words ran an uncomfortable chill down Sheryl's spine. "A captain of the football team skip his ten-year reunion? Why, he'd be more likely to miss his own funeral."

"There's the old class president, Greg Stewart." Sheryl looked to the table where Dawn pointed and still saw traces of the studious young boy in the man with wavy brown hair and metal-rimmed glasses. She recognized some of the faces that surrounded him, forming almost exactly the same closely knit group they had in school.

"Let's join them. Maybe they'll know something about Corry."

"Pull up a chair, ladies." Greg introduced his wife, Susan. Sheryl glanced around the table, searching for some of Corry's friends, but did not see petite and pretty Tina, who had once been his girl, nor his best friend, Rudy.

"Has anyone seen Rudy Fletcher?" Dawn poised her lips in a Marilyn Monroe imitation. "And what about Corry? Does anyone know if he's still as handsome as he used to be?"

Smiles, all around the table, stopped. Metal glinted from Greg's steel-rimmed glasses, obscuring his brown eyes as he finally spoke. "Then you two haven't heard about the accident."

"Accident?" Dawn echoed, her own exuberance fading.

"A head-on collision. It happened a couple years ago. Rudy Fletcher was killed."

Sheryl acknowledged the numbness of shock, but could feel no real sorrow. In school, Rudy and Corry had been inseparable. They even resembled each other, except Rudy was thinner, his hair shades darker. An image of Rudy with his lank brown hair and eyes that always seemed to bore right through her came to mind.

"Corry's wife Tina was in the car, too. She was hurt pretty badly," Greg said.

"What about Corry?" Sheryl asked, breathless.

"You know what a charmed life he's always led. The others in the accident were killed or seriously injured and he got off Scot-free." Greg finished with a frown. "But I hear he and Tina divorced soon after. Maybe he's not taking it as well as it seems. Last time I saw him…he'd been drinking and…he wasn't the same, not at all."

Sheryl's fingers tightened about the wine glass. She had imagined that Corry's life had continued as smooth and unblemished as it had been in school. Instead, fate had dealt him his share of misfortune. She felt the tug of some unidentifiable emotion deep inside of her and quickly hardened her heart against it.

"Do you think he'll be here tonight?" Sheryl asked grimly.

"He'll turn up, all right," Greg replied with confidence.

Sheryl felt the brush of her purse against her leg beneath the table and thought of the gun nestled inside. She would leave it up to fate. If he did appear tonight, let it be a sign.

The buzz of voices around her no longer seemed to connect. Excusing herself, Sheryl wandered away from the table. Outside, a band was busy setting up in the corner of the school lawn. Balloons tied to the bicycle railings waved in the warm evening breeze. The program promised dancing out under the stars. To some, it might have been a pretty scene, but for Sheryl it was spoiled by memories as dark and as thick as the tangles of trees and bushes beyond the stadium walls.

Now, once again, Sheryl saw herself waiting after the game, hoping to catch a glimpse of Corry, her hero, coming from the field. In her memory, she sighed, lost once more in daydreams about him. She thought of the heavy silver eagle's head ring he always wore and imagined him giving it to her, a token of their going steady. An empty dream—by the end of the year it would probably be hanging on a chain around Tina's neck.

Like someone watching a horror movie, Sheryl saw herself crossing the stadium. Sheryl longed to cry out a warning to the shadow image of herself that moved innocently into the dark copse of trees. But she was as powerless to change the scenario as a spectator who sits and watches the screen in a darkened theater.

Someone came out of the locker room. Sheryl turned. She stopped to wait. Something didn't seem quite right. A shivering began deep inside her as the shadowy figure dressed in dark pants and T-shirt moved toward her. "Is that you? Corry? C-Corry?"

Fear began, a heavy thumping in her heart, the urge to run. She began to move away, but a strange sort of fascination slowed her down. The figure overtaking her had no face. She remembered seeing the purple glow of the helmet before the moonlight was completely obscured by the trees.

Sheryl had just turned the dark corner when she had felt rough hands pulling her down into the bushes. Clawing fingers tore at her clothing. She tried to scream but a heavy palm clamped down on her mouth. As his other hand clenched into a fist, ready to strike her, she caught a gleam of a thick, silver ring.

Her assailant's helmet had been removed, but something dark remained over the face, obscuring his features. But she knew who he was. Her last image before a black curtain slipped over her world was two tiny eyes staring down, mocking her. The stone eyes of the eagle, the ring, Corry's ring.

* * *

Grateful that the restroom was empty, Sheryl drew out some paper towels and wiped at her sweat-drenched skin. Then, in an effort to calm herself, she collapsed into one of the stalls and covered her face with her hands.

She didn't know how long she sat huddled in that stall, unable to cry, unable to move or make a sound. The sudden slam of a door startled her. Realizing she had left her purse on the sink ledge, she hurried out. But it was only Dawn, primping in front of the mirror.

"God, I look a mess!" Dawn peered critically at her own image. Intent upon her own reflection, Dawn seemed not to notice Sheryl's distraught mood. "My hair just doesn't look right this color." She made a face at the glass. "Maybe I should have stayed a brunette."

"Nonsense," Sheryl pacified. "You were born to be a blonde."

Dawn paused to spritz her hair with a thick, gel-like spray. Then she said, "Corry's here."

A pounding started in Sheryl's heart. Dawn prepared to leave, but turned as Sheryl called her back. "Dawn, don't tell him you saw me."

Dawn listened curiously as Sheryl explained, "I want to surprise him. But I'll need your help."

Dawn lingered, intrigued, anxious to help rekindle what she probably imagined to be the flames of an old romance. "What is it you want me to do?"

"When the music starts, ask him to dance."

Dawn shrugged. "That should be easy enough. What then?"

"Then get him to take a walk with you on that isolated path behind the stadium. You know the one I mean."

A strange, hurt look crossed Dawn's face. "Why there?"

"It was a...special place for us." Sheryl said with a touch of irony.

Dawn's smile was a little too bright. "It's just that, well, Rudy and the guys used to take me there sometimes after the games. They got me drunk, sort of passed me around." The smile creased into a grimace of pain. "Sex...that's all Rudy and the others ever wanted me for...thought I was too dumb to figure it out."

Sheryl touched her shoulder, feeling a kindred sympathy for the girl who had paid such a price for popularity. "I'm sorry."

Dawn shook back her gel-stiffened hair. "Hey, that was a long time ago. Now, what do you want me to do next?"

"When you get past the stadium, just slip away and leave us alone together." She touched a finger to her lips. "Not a word to him now. I'll be waiting out under the trees."

After Dawn left, Sheryl reached for her purse and her mouth went dry. She resisted the urge to open it, to feel the cold barrel of the gun lying inside.

As Sheryl slipped outside, she stole a single glance toward the table where Greg, Dawn, and the others mingled, and she saw Corry sitting like a king in their midst.

Not exactly the Corry she remembered, but a dark-suited stranger. From the shadows, she observed him, coldly, clinically, as an uncaring doctor might observe an ill patient. He had hollowed out around the shoulders and thickened through the waist. His hair was slightly thinner, a little less golden. But the frigid blue eyes were startlingly the same.

How many times had she silently relived in her bed with Ross the anguish, the humiliation of being raped? Her stony endurance, her pushing him away had finally been the ruination of her marriage. Because of Corry she had seen her one chance for happiness with Ross blow away like the head of a dandelion. Wasn't it only fair that he pay?

* * *

Music played in the cool summer night. Sheryl heard the sound of rustling bushes, the murmur of voices as Corry and Dawn came down the path toward her. "I should have known you'd want to come out here," she heard Corry say. "Brings back old times, doesn't it, Babe?"

She heard Dawn's laughter, then Corry calling out in surprise, "Hey! Where are you going?"

"I'll be back," she heard Dawn reply. "Just wait right here."

As soon as Dawn was out of sight, Sheryl stepped out of the shadows to confront Corry. The two of them were a long way from the lights and music. And they were alone.

Corry squinted his eyes and gaped at her through the darkness as if seeing a ghost. She saw him staring aghast at the livid birthmark in the moonlight. "My God, it's you!" he gasped finally.

"We have a score to settle," Sheryl stated coldly.

His form before her wavered and blurred. The person standing there wasn't Corry, not the virile, handsome football star she remembered. The years had stripped him of his identity as cleanly as a snake sheds its skin. Nothing left, not even the polo shirts. Only the ice-blue eyes.

As if he realized she intended to exact some kind of revenge, Corry put out a hand to her. "Sheryl, listen! It wasn't me that night."

"What do you mean?"

She had expected him to apologize, to plead, but nothing had prepared her for this flat denial.

"It was Rudy. He told me so. How he covered his face and dressed up in my clothes and followed you..."

His outthrust hand made a pleading gesture. And then from his finger she caught the glint of silver, the tiny, glittering pinpoints of light from the eagle's eyes. The ring. Corry's ring.

Rage, cold and silent, pounded in her ears like the roaring of the sea.

"You coward!"

Sheryl fumbled in her purse for the gun. And in that one, dark space of a moment, just before her hands closed around emptiness, Sheryl knew she couldn't go through with it. For her own sake, not his, she knew she couldn't pull the trigger.

The sound of a single shot filled the air.

Corry staggered a little, looking sick, his face stunned. Then he slumped to the ground.

Sheryl heard the sound of Dawn's hysterical sobbing, sobbing that sounded almost like laughter, as the gun slid from her hand. "It was Corry, all right. I knew the bastard raped you. He used to laugh about it when he was drunk. They all used to laugh about it...just like they used to laugh about me."

From far away, the music stopped. Sheryl wondered how long it would be before she heard the wail of sirens. "I suspected what you planned all along," Dawn said, "and when I found the gun I knew...knew you'd never have the guts to go through with it."

"You took the gun from my purse in the restroom. But why, Dawn. Why?"

"For me," Dawn said softly. "I did it for me."

The Drifter
By Loretta Jackson

Basil's racket is to work down and outers on his farm and refuse to pay them...until he runs across a man called Driftwood.

Basil pulled the battered pickup to a stop a little ahead of the hitchhiker and watched as the man ran to catch up. He climbed into the truck and placed a soiled paper sack—probably a change of clothes, a razor—between them on the seat. They drove a while in silence.

"Where are you headed?" Basil asked.

"South," the hitchhiker said.

"Any hurry to get there? Got some work at the farm needs done. Could use a hand. I'll pay one dollar an hour above minimum wage."

Interest glinted in gray eyes. "Sounds fair. I could use some cash."

Basil had no intention of paying out any money. Whenever the time came that the hitchhiker began demanding pay, he'd simply say, "You got food and board. That's all I said I'd give you. If you don't like it, clear out. Or else I'll call the sheriff."

None of them ever brought suit against him, never had money enough for a lawyer or status enough to be believed. Basil couldn't do all the work himself; he couldn't afford to hire help. The only way a person could make a decent living the way farm prices were now was by careful plotting. His schemes worked successfully again and again.

No one ever guessed, although Tedrow, his neighbor to the north, often wondered. "Don't keep help long, do you?"

"Hire too many transients," Basil would grumble. "No good devils. Leave me when I need them most."

Basil cast a glance at the man beside him. He looked harder, older than most of the men he conned. This man was well into middle age, but still strong. Looked as if he might know enough to repair the combine. He was sober, uncommunicative. Something about the set of his thick, dry lips made Basil a little uneasy.

He was glad the man would be sleeping so far from the house. "You stay in the room off the barn," Basil said. The hitchhiker didn't ask for an advance the way most of them did, so Basil's ready excuse went unused. "What do they call you?"

"They call me...Driftwood," the man said.

Damn funny he wouldn't give a decent name, even if he had to make one up. Not that it mattered. It didn't make any difference to Basil what his name was. He was just hands on the other side of heavy loads, a body to drive the tractor.

"I start working at six o'clock. Breakfast at five-thirty. Come through the back door. Leads to the kitchen."

Run down, Driftwood thought, as he headed across the field to the house for breakfast the next morning. Too bad, with a little care, it could be nice.

So could Basil's wife. She had wide blue eyes with big black pupils, the kind that made him want to look again. With all that thick brown hair, she had been pretty. Could be yet, if it wasn't for the fact that she looked so despairing, so exhausted. Basil didn't introduce them. Driftwood said, "Hello," as he seated himself at the table.

She avoided looking at him.

Basil had been applying oil to a battered .22 revolver, which now lay beside his plate. He edged it toward the center of the table, saying, "This gun belonged to my daddy. Shot an intruder with it once."

Driftwood was used to most people's fear of him. The presence of the gun or the warning did not even draw any reaction from him.

"Want you to take a look at the old combine," Basil said. "We'll see if we can get it running."

Driftwood nodded confidently. There was nothing he couldn't get running.

"Hurry and eat," Basil said, pushing the bread toward him.

Homemade, with a butcher knife sticking through the top of it. Driftwood's large hand gripped the faded handle. The once thick metal had worn down, but was honed razor-sharp. He cut off a slice of bread.

Driftwood's eyes wandered to the yellowish stains on the ceiling, followed the streaks down the faded wallpaper. The dilapidated kitchen was bad enough, but the air that hung over it made it worse. Mean and stingy. Driftwood felt uncomfortable, although he ate the eggs and bread with a deliberate slowness.

Elva didn't like most of the drifters Basil brought home, so it didn't matter to her that Basil used them, cheated them. Whenever he was involved in his fraudulent plots, he was preoccupied and did not take his frustrations out on her.

The men had worked in the field until dark. Now Basil was in the front room going over accounts. Driftwood had finished the evening meal long ago, but he still sat at the table. Elva could feel his eyes fastened on her.

"That your kid?" Driftwood asked.

Elva had pinned his picture—that of a plump baby—on a nail near the stove, so she could look at it while she cooked. Once her son had become as tall as Basil, the fighting had started. Finally, before he was grown, he had run away. The boy's leaving had completed the utter ruination of her life. She thought he was somewhere in California, but she never heard a word from him.

Elva felt like one of those mice she often caught in a trap that spasmodically struggled to live. Even if Elva pulled free, she knew by this time she had been mortally wounded.

So year after year passed and Elva worked, mending the same clothes, mopping the same worn linoleum, trying to shut out Basil's increasing list of gripes.

Elva never stood up to him, not even when he struck her. She never answered his complaints, only to herself. How could she get threadbare material to hold together? How could she make decent meals out of nothing?

She had spells of hating Basil. They were periodic, intense, like headaches, only there was nothing she could take to dull them.

"Let me help you with that." Driftwood took the heavy mop bucket from her with quick ease. She watched the strong brown hands squeeze out the rag.

"Sit down, little lady," he said in a kindly way. "Old Driftwood is going to show you how to mop a floor."

* * *

"It's the third. I've worked here a month," Driftwood said. "I need to buy some things."

"I'll pay you the first of August," Basil answered. His slight smile had an ugly edge. "Even give you a big bonus. Be worth your while to stay."

"That won't do."

"I just can't come up with the cash now. Until someone pays me. If that's not good enough for you..." Basil wasn't speaking forcefully, the way he usually did. He even shrugged, something Driftwood had never seen him do. "Then I guess you'll just have to leave."

Driftwood said nothing. He had been suspicious of Basil from the first, so he wasn't the least bit surprised by his intentions, or even very angry. He turned and walked across the dusty field to the bare room adjoining the barn.

Driftwood didn't show up for work the next morning. When Basil knocked on his door, Driftwood called, "Since you don't have the money to pay me, I think I'll stay in bed."

For days Driftwood hung around the farm, appearing without much effort to be frightening and sinister. With money from his decreasing funds he bought food, which he ate in his room. He said not a word to either Basil or Elva.

Driftwood knew his immovable presence was beginning to take its toll on Basil. Basil's hands shook whenever they met face to face, and he seemed unable to muster the nerve for a confrontation.

It rained all day Friday, and Driftwood remained in his room, stretched out on the hard cot. Long toward evening an angry pounding sounded from outside, causing the half-rotten wall near his bed to vibrate. Basil began yelling threats about his trespassing, about calling the sheriff.

By the time Driftwood opened the door, Basil was nowhere in sight. Not only a bully, but a coward, too. He preyed only on the weak and helpless.

Basil did not return until the next evening. This time his fists on the door possessed a sort of frustrated frenzy. Driftwood remained inside making no move and no reply.

Two days later Driftwood returned from town to find his room locked and barred. Pinned to the door at eye level, a note, scrawled in Basil's sloppy hand, read, "I can't put up with this anymore."

As Driftwood held the message in his hand, a smile stretched his thick lips. He lifted the soiled paper bag, filled with his belonging, which Basil had set outside the locked door, and tucking Basil's note into his breast pocket, started away.

Before leaving, he thought, he might just walk across the long, dusty field and say goodbye to Elva.

At the doorway to the kitchen, he stopped. Elva was standing over Basil, who was sprawled on the floor. She clutched tightly with both hands the .22 revolver, the one that had belonged to Basil's father. How long had she been standing over him like that, the gun barrel pointed at his lifeless body?

Driftwood had observed the way Basil always vented his anger on his wife, the way he made Elva's existence a living hell. For a moment he felt an intense pity for her and thought about how surprised Basil must have been when one of his tirades met with opposition.

Elva seemed totally incapable of any movement. Driftwood's eyes lowered to the blood that streamed across Basil's face unto the pale yellow linoleum.

Elva's black pupils seemed to blot out all the blue. Her white, terrified face caused him to straighten up, as if in self-defense. Driftwood wasn't educated, but he had survival sense. In the frightened depths of Elva's wild eyes, he could see her thoughts.

He had seen the same look before on other desperate faces. She was thinking how easy it would be to remove her fingerprints from the weapon, to blame him, a no-good, a drifter, for her husband's death. Driftwood could almost hear her testifying to her husband's misdeeds, deeds that would give him motive. At first Driftwood started backing out of the kitchen, then he changed his mind and came forward.

He took the gun from her and carefully wiped the prints with the tea towel he found on the table, then bent and pressed the revolver into Basil's hand.

Driftwood rose, gazed at Elva in silence. He took Basil's note from his breast pocket, scanning, as he did, the desperate words scrawled in Basil's own hand, "I can't put up with this anymore." He placed the paper, ripped from some old notebook, on the kitchen table where Basil usually sat.

Driftwood left the house hurriedly, crossing the great expanse of field to the highway. Once he thought he heard Elva call his name, but he did not slow his steps or look back.

After several attempts to catch a ride, a late-model car pulled to a stop. Driftwood climbed inside.

"Where are you going?"

"West."

The driver was dressed expensively, but Driftwood noted the shoddiness present in the red-rimmed eyes, in the sagging lines of weak mouth. Driftwood watched him out of the corner of his eye, just as he had watched Basil. The way people were these days, he thought, it pays to be leery.

Mirror Image
By Vickie Britton

Unfailingly, a stranger, grim and watchful, occupies the front row of Roc's concerts...is he a living threat or an apparition from out of Roc's sullied past?

The Dark Star vibrated with flashing lights and heavy metal music. The smoke-filled tavern with its live band drew a huge night crowd. To Roc, it was just another place to play.

Inside the tiny dressing room Roc hunched in a chair in front of the mirror. He smiled at his smoky reflection. The image in the dingy glass smirked back at him, tinted a hazy pink from the lighting.

The man in the mirror didn't look the least bit happy. His face appeared unhealthily gaunt and shadowed. His lips were thick, sensual, his nose slightly wide, giving him a coarse, animal-look that he knew women found attractive. His mouth stretched into a smile, a mechanical one...a stage smile. He practiced once again. Better, he thought. Yes, he was going to be able to get through tonight.

"Come on," Jake the drummer called. An impatient rap sounded on the door. "Five minutes and we're on!"

Five more minutes. Roc gazed back into the mirror intently, as if searching for something he couldn't quite see. The face that stared back at him now seemed older than his years, worldly. The black eyes possessed a slight glaze, but not enough so Jake would notice.

Turning away from the mirror, Roc opened a dresser drawer and rummaged frantically until his hand finally closed upon a little white vial. Two more wouldn't hurt. Almost ill with nervousness, he shook a couple of the pills out into his hand and swallowed them. Then he closed his eyes and took a deep breath. He wished he could eliminate these moments before he went on stage. He always felt tense, wired. In fact, if it wasn't for the pills sometimes he didn't think he could get through the performance at all.

A banging sounded again. "We're on, man."

Roc loosened the neck of his ebony shirt and pushed back long black hair that fell nearly to his shoulders. Then he stepped out to meet Jake, feeling suddenly very confident.

On stage, Roc was aware of nothing but the surging music, the pounding of wild rhythm in his brain. He clenched the mike in his hands and moved his body to the pulse of drums and electric guitar. He sang and screamed, moving wildly across the stage. His teeth flashed white and his hair shook with every movement. He gave himself up totally to the music, free and uninhibited, barely conscious of the dancing, swaying crowd.

Toward the end of the song, he noticed the stranger. The man, always clad in an elegant, well-tailored suit, had been at his last few gigs. He did not join the dancing. He always sat alone at the same table near the front. The man's face, hazy in the flickering lights, the eyes, sad and a little reproachful, gave Roc a strange, choked feeling.

The man obviously didn't belong here. The conservative gray of his suit, his neat hair, cut in a moderate length, made not the slightest concession to the seamy atmosphere with its harsh music and flashing lights. In fact, he looked totally out of place, the way Roc himself might have looked several years ago.

The stranger caught his gaze and held it. Something about the man's presence gave Roc the feeling of owing an old debt, long forgotten, nevertheless unpaid. Rock owed lots of people money. Did he owe this man? No...Roc had the feeling this was about something entirely different. The man's eyes, the penetrating way they followed Roc, unnerved him. He got the strangest feeling that they could see into his very soul.

The band started to warm up for another number. Everything, including the stranger, was forgotten in the mad, primitive beat. Again, cheers and applause thundered. Roc's heart pounded, and he was bathed in sweat as he left the stage.

After a change of clothing, Roc went down to the bar and ordered a drink. He found a nearby table and sat alone, savoring the fiery liquid that burned his dry throat. The chair beside him scraped.

"May I join you, Robert?"

The way the stranger addressed him sent a chill down his spine. Why, no one had called him Robert since his innocent childhood days.

Roc frowned. "Have we met before?" he asked, a little abruptly.

"You surely must know me, Robert," the stranger replied with patient tolerance. Robert again. Why couldn't Roc remember him? He searched the stranger's face, but recognized nothing familiar. Still, he couldn't afford to be rude. This might be some kind of talent scout checking out the band. "You must like our music," he said. "This is the third time you've been here to see us play."

"My business is only with you," the stranger replied. His long, thin fingers tapped upon the table until Roc wanted to force him to stop. With a look that seemed critical, judgmental, he added, "By the way, I didn't enjoy the music."

His words caused a sudden flare of resentment and anger. "Then why are you here? Who are you, anyway?"

The man looked disappointed. "You haven't got a clue, do you?" He hesitated a moment, then added with an elusive smile, "But don't worry. We shall get to know each other very well."

The stranger rose and without another word drifted away. With a puzzled shake of his head, Roc finished his drink.

The following weeks, the band traveled, making a wide circuit. The stranger never missed a night. What could he gain by hearing the same show over and over, a show he said he didn't even like? Roc wondered nervously how he always managed, no matter where they played, to get a table right in front. Whoever he was, the man must have influence.

One night, after the show, Roc and Don, the lead guitarist, sat having a drink.

"What a night!" Don rubbed a hand through his thick blond beard. "If this keeps up, we're gonna be rich, man!"

Roc's thoughts were preoccupied. His eyes roamed around the room. About two tables away sat the gray-clad stranger. He waved his hand slightly as Roc glanced toward him. God, but that man did give him the creeps. Why was he constantly hounding him?

"You know that character?" Roc demanded of Don. He pointed directly toward the stranger. "He hasn't missed one of our gigs since the Dark Star."

"No kidding?"

"He's always staring at me like that. Always watching. See? He's doing it now. And that suit he's wearing! He's always dressed like that."

"Say, you don't think he's one of those talent scouts, do you?" Don asked. "Sure hope so." He glanced about casually.

"Where is this dude you're talking about, anyway?"

"You're looking right at him."

"What guy? I don't see any guy." Don gave Roc a curious look.

"Two tables up from us. Surely you must see him!"

Roc started to point in his direction, but the stranger, rising, smiled and left.

Saturday night a party at the beach followed the last show. Roc arrived later than the rest, and at eleven o'clock, the shoreline was crowded. The music played full blast. Some people had gone for a moonlight swim. Most of the rest huddled in small groups, talking and drinking.

Don greeted Roc with enthusiasm. "Wild party, man. It's about time you got here."

A pretty, dark-haired girl in a white bikini wandered up beside them. Don turned to Roc, saying, "Meet Barbara."

The girl smiled and took Roc's hand. "You can call me Baby. Everyone else does."

"I'm—"

She stopped his introduction. "Everyone knows Roc Devlon."

She tugged on his arm. "Let's go swimming."

Roc stripped to his trunks and for a while they swam side by side in the cold water.

Later, they waded on the beach, wandering far from the party until they came to a secluded place where they could be alone. Roc and the girl sank down together upon the sand. He kissed her deeply, passionately, then he froze.

Someone was watching them. Roc broke away quickly. He stood, peering out into the darkness, not knowing what he expected to see.

"Roc, what's wrong?" the girl asked, a quiver of fear in her voice.

"I don't know." He looked around. What had he sensed that had unnerved him so?

Then he saw the man, near the rocks. Staring. Forever staring at Roc with those wide, hypnotic eyes. Even from here, Roc could feel their sad, disappointed gaze boring into his very soul. The stranger's hair was ruffled and windblown and the moonlight illuminated the silvery material of his suit making him seem to glow with eerie phosphorescence. Slowly, the figure turned and began to drift away toward the water.

"Wait!" Roc cried angrily. "Who are you? What do you want?" But the man kept on walking, ignoring his anguished shouts.

Barbara was on her feet beside him, looking frightened. "Who are you talking to? What's happening?"

"Oh, my God!"

"Roc?"

"Leave me alone!" Roc sank to the sand and remained there, motionless.

"What's wrong with you?" He barely heard Barbara's anxious demand for answers. He picked up handfuls of sand and clenched and unclenched his fingers, feeling it sift out of his grasp and back on to the beach. Finally, Barbara walked off. Later, Roc got up and went back to the party. Barbara, now on Don's arm, watched him with hurt eyes. He didn't care about her anyway, so the fact that she was with Don didn't even bother him. He didn't care about any of them. He just wanted to be alone.

Friday night rolled around. The band had traveled to a neighboring town where they were scheduled to play at a small club. With apprehension his dark eyes skimmed the crowd. He felt overwhelmed with relief when he saw that the stranger was nowhere in sight. The place he always occupied at one of the front tables remained empty.

Roc was beginning to think that maybe it had just been coincidence that the man had appeared everywhere he went. As he sang, the music loosened his tension. Then he looked out into the crowd for a brief second. A pair of intense eyes locked with his. In the previously empty seat, bathed in glowing light, the stranger sat watching him with that infernal depth to his gaze.

Roc's hands began to shake. It was as if the man had appeared out of nowhere. Suddenly, Roc could stand no more. He rushed from the stage with a half-cry of terror.

Roc was trembling uncontrollably as he reached the backstage room. He fumbled for his pills and was about to swallow three of them when he heard someone come up behind him.

"What made you run off like that, Roc? The crowd thought it was part of the act. But we never planned it."

Trying to hide the pills from Don, he pushed the bottle back in the drawer. He was too late.

"You had better stop taking those before you kill yourself."

After a long silence, Roc said, "It's not what you think, Don. I'm not stoned."

"Then what is it? What is bothering you?"

"That man. He was there again. He's always staring at me. Always there!"

"What man?" Don gave Roc a worried look.

"What's happening to me, Don? Am I seeing things? Am I going crazy?"

Don's gaze drifted to the drawer where Roc had hidden the pills. "I think you need a break from all this pressure."

"I don't want—"

"We need you in the band, Roc. But you've got to pull yourself together." In a voice that left no room for argument, he insisted, "Why don't you skip the next few nights? Jake will cover for you. Just take it easy, get some rest. We'll see you next Friday."

* * *

Roc didn't feel like going back to his empty hotel room. Instead, he bought a ticket to a late-night movie. It was a comedy, but Roc didn't laugh, not once. He stared blankly at the screen, not really caring what the movie was about. When it finally came to an end and people began to stream from the theater, Roc wished it wasn't over. He hesitated then got up to leave.

As he moved down the corridor with the crowd, he thought he saw a familiar form, a flash of well-groomed hair, of neat gray suit. Had the man followed him here? Roc tried to block the thought from his mind. He had to get back to his room. He had to get some sleep. Then everything would be all right.

Once in his hotel room, Roc greedily drank a bottle of wine. His nerves were shattered. He crawled into bed without bothering to undress and switched on the radio. A song played soft and hauntingly, not the loud, fast-moving stuff he always enjoyed. Drugged by the wine, he fell into a troubled sleep.

Roc woke in the middle of the night to the sound of the radio sputtering and hissing. He felt a sense of panic and for a moment had trouble remembering who and where he was. He fumbled for the radio knob and the room clicked into deathly silence.

An uneasy feeling made him rise and go to the window. The streetlight threw a soft glow on the alley below. Just beneath where a lone, dark form was moving down the narrow walkway. Terror filled Roc, then rage as he watched the solitary figure pace back and forth, as if waiting for him.

Pushed to the breaking point, half out of his mind with fear, he jerked out the drawer of a nearby nightstand. The contents clattered to the floor. He groped in the semi-darkness until his fingers closed upon the handle of the switchblade he always kept nearby. The metal gleamed ugly and wicked in the faint light.

He rushed through the corridor and bounded down the back steps. When he reached the alley, the man turned toward him and smiled.

"Now," Roc cried. "Maybe you will tell me why you follow me around everywhere I go!" The knife in his hand shook uncontrollably. "Who the hell are you? What do you want? What do you want from me?"

The man did not appear shocked or surprised by Roc's screaming confrontation. The smile remained; he looked mildly amused. "Do you really think you can destroy me?"

"Damn you!" With a savage, almost inhuman cry Roc thrust the knife deep into the heart of his tormenter. The man's face blurred before him. Roc glanced fearfully around, grateful for the darkness, the silence. No one had seen. No one had heard.

Roc, as if in a trance, stared down at the crumpled form on the ground beneath him. The man's eyes were still staring, but this time they were empty. A crimson splotch was already spreading across the front of his crisp, white shirt.

"Oh, my God." Roc half-whispered, half-whimpered, into the still night. But he knew what he had to do. With a burst of super-human energy, he dragged the body behind an old shed in the back of the hotel. Finding a shovel, he buried the body deep in the patch of woods beyond the alleyway.

Roc spent the next day in his room in a state of near shock. That evening he ventured out to get the papers and anxiously watched the news. No mention was made of discovering a body. It could be months, even years, before he was found. There had been no witnesses. Roc was certain that there was no way the murder could ever be traced to him.

Roc felt no remorse for what he had done. No sorrow. No guilt. His crime seemed unreal, as if it hadn't really happened at all. He felt shaken...yet oddly relieved. The tour had gone full circle and tomorrow he would be back at the Dark Star.

* * *

The performance was about to start. Roc appeared composed as he peered at his reflection in the backstage mirror. He was a little paler than usual, and his eyes were slightly shadowed with black. But everything was going to be all right.

"We're on, Roc," came the call from Jake, the drummer.

Roc smiled, suddenly self-assured. Tonight would be a great success. He could feel it.

He walked out on the stage, shook back his hair and introduced the first number.

The band started playing. Roc glanced casually over the audience. His eyes strayed automatically to the place in the front row near the floodlights where the stranger usually sat. The seat was vacant.

He began to sing. Suddenly, from the corner of his eye, he saw the side door open. Or was he imagining it? Surely this couldn't be happening! No one was allowed in once the performance had started. But when the door crept slowly open, wider and wider, nobody turned around to look. No one else seemed to notice.

Roc stopped singing and watched in horror. His eyes widened with disbelief and terror as the familiar gray-clad figure slowly limped in. His chest was smeared with blood. His pale hand clutched a deep red spot, a spot that even as Roc watched, was beginning to fade, to disappear.

The well-dressed man, no longer a stranger, calmly took his seat.

Date with a Stranger
Loretta Jackson

Linda thinks nothing ever happens in Claytonville...until one terrible night.

W ould the rest of my life be like this—cold and empty? Linda slipped off her blue suit jacket, placing it carefully over the arm of the platform rocker, and walked woodenly toward the refrigerator. Sometimes the awful solitude didn't bother her, but tonight a deadly weariness washed over her as liquid as water.

Even though she didn't want to eat, Linda took out the leftover meat loaf and automatically switched on the TV, hoping the formal voice of the news anchor would qualify as warmth and companionship. She didn't often allow herself to give in to depression, but the long evening ahead, without even the usual work she brought home from the office, seemed to court it.

The ringing phone startled her. She eyed it skeptically, letting it ring again before she lifted the receiver. "Hello, this is Linda Bryan."

"You work at Simpkin's Supply? You're Ross Simpkin's secretary?"

Linda tried to place the deep male voice, refined, polite, a bit unsure. "That's right."

He hesitated a moment, as though he didn't know how to continue, then said quickly, "You don't know me. Actually, you've probably never even seen me. I've only been in Claytonville a week. I'm working for Ross Simpkin, too, but over at the warehouse."

Silently she waited for him to go on.

"This town is so quiet, so lonesome. I thought maybe if...if I could get acquainted with someone...maybe we could go to a movie tonight?"

Linda wanted to say "Yes!" Anything would be better than this feeling of despair she had tonight. But she wasn't a girl, she was thirty-four years old, and by this time caution and reserve were firmly a part of her. Again she waited.

"I realize this is unusual. I should have dropped by the office and introduced myself. I intended to. If you don't want to meet me like this, I'll understand—but it's so confounded quiet tonight. I really think I'll go crazy with no one to talk to." He paused, as if ashamed for having said so much. "Are you still there?"

"Why, yes, I am."

"I've wanted to work up the courage to ask you out ever since I first laid eyes on you. Please forgive me, but it's much easier on the phone." Another pause. "Would you go out tonight? Wings of Love is playing at the Grand."

"Well..." Linda could feel doubt creeping into her voice. Suddenly angry with herself, she said, "Why not?"

"Good girl! Now, where can I meet you?"

"How about the park? It's right on my way to town." She glanced at her watch. "I'll be there at eight-thirty, and we can catch the second show."

"You won't know me, but I'll know you. I'll come up and introduce myself. Goodbye now, and don't forget—eight-thirty in the park, next to the swings." The last hurried words were followed by a click at the other end of the line.

Actually, Linda hadn't meant down in the park, but on the sidewalk that ran by it. But what difference could that make? Nothing ever happened in Claytonville. Anyway, she had no way to call him up and change it. She realized for the first time that she didn't even know his name.

Letting the receiver fall into place, Linda felt sadness drop away from her. Had she just dreamed this answer to a prayer, this date with a stranger?

Just a half hour! She selected her best aqua dress and the high heels she almost never wore. What would he look like? She guessed, as she ran a comb through her already neat dark hair. He would be tall. Thin. Handsome. She could tell by his voice. And, of course, blond. It was the blond men who usually noticed her.

She took a final look at herself in the mirror: straight nose, only a trifle long; wide, gray eyes that looked truthful and earnest; trim figure. She even felt pretty.

Linda's hand shook as she sprayed on cologne. Will he like me? What if he doesn't?

The old caution returned the moment she stepped outside the apartment. A logical voice from inside demanded: what's wrong with you? How can you be willing, like a common tramp, to meet someone you've never so much as laid eyes on! And of all places, in that dark ravine Claytonville calls a park.

Linda refused to respond to the voice. She hadn't felt so young and happy in a long time. The memory of his voice sent a thrill of romance, of youth, through her. After his call, she admitted to herself that she could not spend the evening alone.

She looked for the moon, but clouds covered it and left everything dark. As she began walking the three blocks to the park, she thought about Claytonville. It was a small, unfriendly town, clannish, as only a little town can be that had long ago stopped growing.

Linda had lived here for seven years and had almost no friends. Ross Simpkin and his staff at work had their own social set, their evenings and weekends busy with small interests that never varied, with their own families.

She didn't blame them, and she didn't try to be included. She sought no one out, met only those people daily routine forced her to meet. Actually, the only one in Claytonville she thought of as friend was the old night watchman, Dave Porter. He always chatted, inquired about her problems and understood her.

Linda's thoughts leaped ahead. She wondered what this stranger who waited for her would say when they finally stood face to face.

Only occasionally a car would pass. Not a person was on the streets, no one on his front porch—not one sound of voice or laughter. One would think it was midnight instead of just eight-thirty.

The park, overhung with trees, was a mass of shadows. She looked down into the deep ravine, but all detail was lost in darkness. How could she go through with it? The park was deserted, foreboding. The very sight of the flagstone steps descending into blackness sent a cold chill through her. She turned and walked away. She should never have come in the first place.

As soon as Linda crossed the street, she caught sight of Dave Porter, who was already on his rounds, probably had already checked most of the business buildings to make sure they were safely locked. He grinned and waved when he saw her. "Nice evening, Linda. You out getting your exercise?"

"Yes, but it's so very dark tonight." She thought momentarily of the steps behind her and shivered. "I was going to the show at the Grand, but I can't make up my mind."

"It's no good. My wife dragged me to it Saturday. It's a silly damned love story where this—"

"Now don't go telling me the end of it, as you usually do." She laughed a little, her fears dispelled by his presence.

"Now when did I ever do that? Just don't get fond of her boyfriend. After he leaves for Rome..." he stopped short. "See, I'm not even going to tell you what kills him."

"Thanks for that."

They talked a while longer, and as Linda watched him walk away, she felt foolish, ashamed of her childish fears. In a good little town like this, with Dave Porter patrolling, how could she be anything but safe?

Confidently she turned back to the park, strode quickly down the rock steps and stood by the swings. A very dim park lamp gave just enough light to see the area close by, but thickness of elms and cottonwoods would have hidden the street above her from view even if it hadn't been for the darkness.

She listened without moving. Sounds of locusts chirping, a slight rustling of leaves, surrounded her. She watched alertly for her date, not wanting to miss the first glimpse of him in the dim light. The feeling suddenly washed over her that she was being watched. Stop being foolish, she told herself. Here she was again acting like a baby, afraid to be alone in the dark. But the feeling persisted.

Linda drew in her breath slowly and straightened up. She wouldn't wait much longer. Just a little while.

After a few uneasy minutes, she checked her watch, strain-ing her eyes to see the dial. She thought it said eight-forty-five, but she couldn't be sure without a better light. Perhaps he was delayed or maybe he changed his mind. Or maybe it had been some practical joker, sitting back in the comfort of his home now and laughing. Convinced that this was the answer, Linda became angry at herself, at the whole absurd situation.

Hearing a noise, she gazed expectantly at the spot it had come from, glad, after all, that he had shown up.

Then she saw him. He came out of the cavelike blackness between the trees. She saw him and stepped back, too choked to even scream.

The very sight of him stopped her breath. All confidence and strength melted from her body, and she could only step back, back, slowly. She could not tear her eyes away from this man.

His thin shoulders hunched, covered by a ragged, dirty shirt. What little light there was illuminated shaggy hair, beard, wide-open staring eyes. She kept stepping stupidly backward, unable to whirl, unable to run.

He stalked forward toward her. His gait changed to a slow, loose shuffle. For every step she took backward, he seemed to take two toward her.

Then he laughed. The laughter was ragged, interspersed by excited catches of breath. It was an uncontrolled sound that froze the blood in her veins.

She had to get away from him. Now able to force her legs to obey her, she whirled and ran. The steps to the top…she must reach them. Terror gave her speed.

Linda could feel the pounding of her heart in her chest, in her throat. She did not reach the steps. He grabbed her. She struggled, striking out with hands, feet, head. But she could not break his grasp. A hand snaked across her throat, choking off her scream, bending her back, back. She saw his face close to her own: his mouth loose, his face lined and grimy. His eyes wide open and irrational.

With every bit of her strength, she fought, clawing, kicking. Fingers clutched her throat tighter, cutting off what breath remained. His hideous, broken laughter sounded everywhere, engulfed her.

Linda could feel herself being dragged along the ground, back into the shadows of looming trees. Helplessly she watched her heels dragging along the path. She knew she couldn't hold out. She was going to faint.

At that instant, she saw an arm encircle the man's neck. His hold around her throat loosened. She pushed herself free, falling hard, half-blinded by tears and gasping for air for her tortured lungs. She could not get up, could not move. She watched the terrible struggle above her, heard the thud of blows, the shuffle of feet on gravel and dirt, and an occasional gasp or muffled curse.

At last she saw her attacker flung to the ground. He cried out as a foot smacked his stomach, then he lay still.

The other man rubbed a hand across his forehead where the madman had scratched him. His breath was short as he hurried toward Linda and gently assisted her to her feet. She saw a lean, handsome face, a shock of curly-blond hair. She had never seen anyone before who looked so fine and good,and so welcome!

She saw the concern in his eyes. "Are you all right?" he asked anxiously.

Linda could not answer. Her eyes followed the trail of blood that wound its way down his face. At last she leaned against him and cried until she could cry no longer.

His arms held her, supporting her and holding her head against his broad, muscular shoulder. "It's all right now," he murmured gently. "It's all over. Everything's OK."

When she found her voice she could only say, "Thank God you happened along! Thank God!"

"It's about time," he answered grimly, shame creeping into his voice. "I was supposed to be here at eight-thirty."

Redemption
By Vicki Britton

Jackal, a phony who cashes in on his tattoo and black leather image, is about to behold the face of true evil.

Death grunge, the latest craze in heavy metal, was Jackal's ticket to the top. He had seen the trend coming and was cashing in good. The black leather, the tattoos and piercings, the whips and chains and phony mutilations...the kids ate it up like nose candy.

Jackal relished it all—the adulation, the mimicry, the indignant outrage of the religious right. But most of all...he loved the power.

Jackal left the chaos behind, slipped through the back door and into a waiting limo to avoid being crushed by a mob of zealous fans.

The chauffeur nodded as Jackal ducked into the limo and they tore off down the highway.

The man behind the wheel was a new driver, nondescript, his thick brown hair clipped short beneath the chauffeur's cap.

Square-jawed, a little heavy set, he had the muscular build of a soldier. He looked like the veteran of some war, but too young for Vietnam, too old for the Persian Gulf.

"Where to?" the chauffeur asked through the open glass partition that separated them. Jackal sensed his veiled contempt. He tried to imagine the man at one of his riotous concerts, replete with drugs and booze, and failed. Chauffeuring this controversial star was just a job to the driver, Jackal sensed, one he carried out with a resigned sense of duty. A cigarette, probably the only sin he would admit to, lay smoldering in the ashtray.

"Back to the hotel, I guess." The spotlights of the huge stadium and all that went with it—the noise, the heat, the pressing crowd, faded into the distance.

The glass window remained open and through the partition Jackal could smell smoke as the man lifted the cigarette to his lips and took a drag, but said nothing. There was something about this new driver that Jackal instinctively didn't like. Jackal, with his long black hair and leather, his piercings and tattoos, was definitely not a person you would want meet in a dark alley. But this guy, he observed wryly, would be more likely to steal your wallet.

What made him think that? Windshield wipers slapped against the glass as they drove on through the rain-spattered night.

"The name's Sam," the driver said. "Sam Jones, just like my father before me. "Course I know yours. Everyone does."

Jackal was glad for the talk, idle talk to fill the miles back to the city.

"My boy David's a real fan of yours. Yep, David's a real nut about this headbanger stuff." The man took a final drag on his cigarette, then stubbed it out in the ashtray. The limo swerved as he reached into his shirt pocket and drew a photograph from his wallet. "This was taken a while back. He's a good kid. The old lady took off about two years ago. Now it's just the boy and me."

Jackal gazed at a younger, brown-haired spitting-image of the driver.

"No offense, but this whole heavy metal scene—the drugs and the violence. I don't get it."

"It's just music." Jackal shrugged. "What's to understand?"

"Why you guys are always taking the names of murderers for one thing," the man said. "Seems strange to me to glorify a serial killer, that's all. That joker who calls himself Manson, after Charles Manson, for example. And I hear one of these shock-mongers is calling himself Gacy and another Ramirez." After a moment's pause, he added, "I remember the Jackal. Worst of all. The way he killed those women...made Jack the Ripper look like an amateur. Got the chair, which is exactly what he deserved." He turned and craned his neck as if to see Jackal's reaction.

"It's just a name."

"Why keep the memory of such evil alive?"

"Who'd come to see Lou Scwartz play?"

Sam grinned. "That your real name?"

"The one I was born with." He thought for a moment. "In answer to your question, people are attracted to evil. Evil sells."

"It sells, all right. To our impressionable youth." Sam's voice rose slightly and Jackal hoped he wasn't going to get on the soapbox about the destruction of American values. "The darkness, the chaos, it lures them, all right, just like lambs to the slaughter."

A few concerts ago, when Jackal had slashed his arm on the stage, when the fake blood had rained down, a teenager in the crowd had emulated him with a real knife and had to be taken away in an ambulance.

"I'm not hurting anyone. No one's forced to go to my concerts."

"No, they come of their own free will, even pay for the privilege of being brainwashed. I tell you, someone has to be held accountable."

"You one of those born agains?"

"I'm a believer, if that's what you mean. In sin and redemption." He slanted Jackal a look. "But what would you know of all of that? You might even be one of those Devil worshipers."

"I don't believe in anything."

"Nothing?"

"Nothing I can't spend."

This seemed to bother Sam. "Who do you pray to when you are troubled if you don't believe in God?"

"I don't pray."

The lights of the city flashed by as they drove in silence. "My David, he pierced his tongue. Didn't even ask my permission. Damn kids. Who understands them?" Sam shrugged. "I used to be the boy's hero. Now it's you. His room's an absolute shrine to Jackal. Isn't that a riot?"

Jackal leaned forward. "I think you missed the exit to the hotel," he said.

Sam slapped his thigh. "So I did! Hey, I just had an idea. What a surprise it would be if I brought you home with me. Why, my boy'd give his right arm to meet you. Maybe he'd even think his old man was cool. My place isn't far. How about it?"

Jackal started to protest, but then shrugged. Why not? He had nothing planned until much later, until the girls showed up.

Besides, the idea of meeting such a devout admirer flamed his ego. "Always eager to meet a fan."

The driver soon pulled unto a long gravel road that led to a drab brown two-story, as plain and nondescript as the man himself. It could be anyone's house.

Once inside, Jackal was reminded of his father's place after his mother had died, sparsely furnished, surface clean, scattered beer cans a reminder that no woman lived there anymore. From somewhere below them, he could hear the heavy reverberation of music...his music...hammering deep and loud.

"David!" Sam called. He headed for the cabinet where he drew out whiskey and two glasses. "His room's in the basement. That's where he spends all his time."

"Davey," he called again. He turned back to Jackal with the whiskey and shook his head. "It's hopeless. Can't hear anything over that din." Barely giving Jackal time to toss back his whiskey, he moved toward the stairs. "Come on. You'll have to see this to believe it. A shrine, I tell you. An absolute shrine."

A strange sixth sense stole over Jackal, a vague sensation that he was stepping into some sort of carefully laid trap. But, warmed by the whiskey, led by his vanity, he followed Sam down the steps.

As they entered the unfinished basement, Jackal hesitated. The musty darkness reminded him of a story he had read in his youth, wasn't it the *Cask of Amontilado*, something about cellars and wine? Jackal's uneasiness grew. To his recollection, the story hadn't had a happy ending.

As if sensing his apprehension, Sam called out, "This way." They passed a washer and dryer and started down a dark corridor that ended with a closed door. Music, louder now that they were closer to its source, poisoned the air around them.

"This is his room."

Without knocking, Sam turned the knob. From the center of the room a stereo pulsed, a living thing. Colored lights flashed off and on in a zigzag pattern across images of Jackal plastered upon the concrete walls, over the cracked dresser mirror, upon every available space. In one quick glance Jackal saw the tousled, empty bed, the electric guitar propped in one corner...and something else, something that made him look again, as if he were seeing things.

Attached to the far wall, like a prop from one of his stage performances, were instruments of torture and a set of heavy chains.

"What the..."

A sharp, inhuman cry, a cry of anguish and sheer rage made him start to spin around, but before Jackal could fully turn, a fierce blow to the temple silenced him. Jackal slumped to the floor.

When Jackal came to, his wrists were shackled to the wall. In outrage he struggled against the unyielding chain.

"What do you think you're doing?" Panic rose in his voice. "What did you do with the real limo driver? Who the hell are you?"

And suddenly he knew. "David's the one...who slashed himself at that concert."

"That's right. David's dead. He was trying to be like you, trying to be you. Got himself all doped up, slashed his arms with a knife. He bled to death."

"It wasn't my fault. Surely you can't blame me!"

"You were his idol, the center of his whole life. My David believed in you. He thought your act was for real."

"It was only a stage trick! I'm just a showman!"

Sam's voice rose over the roar of deafening music. "Are you telling me my boy died for nothing?"

Jackal lifted his hands and the chains rattled. "Please, just let me go. It wasn't my fault."

"I told you someone must be held accountable."

The man took a menacing step toward him. "Let's see who comes to your rescue...God or the Devil."

Jackal knew his only hope was to somehow appeal to his captor, to throw himself upon his mercy. He knew no one else would hear his screams. "You can't do this! I tell you, I'm not responsible. I didn't even know the boy. My God, what kind of monster are you?"

The driver's eyes glittered as he answered with a sinister smile, "You can call me Son of Sam."

Responsibility
By Loretta Jackson

When Everett isn't responsible for some major disaster, the world is quick to blame him, but what happens when he really is responsible?

"Everett simply refuses to take responsibility for anything," I overheard Marjorie telling Dr. Monett when I finally agreed to check in to Reimer's Foundation for treatment.

Soon I found myself sitting across a huge desk facing this stout, middle-aged psychiatrist. After being well-briefed by my wife, he had no expectations whatsoever that I was going to utter a word.

"Dr. Dondee," he began, "says he finds very little reason for your being here. He says—I have lots of confidence in Dr. Dondee—he says it should be a simple enough matter for you to begin, let's say, being yourself again. Dr. Dondee suggests that we start by chatting about things. How does that sound to you? We'll talk about whatever you want to talk about."

I felt waves of anxiety, as physical as waves in the ocean, separating us, but even as the sad, lined face receded from view, a certain warning rang out: You must talk to him! I started to speak several times before any sound was audible. "My job..."

Startled, encouraged, the doctor leaned forward snatching at my words, "Yes, your job. Go on, Mr. Smith."

"It's a waste of time. They, my students, don't want to learn." I fell into gloomy silence. The first words I had verbalized in months, and all they had accomplished was to create in him that look of earnest doubting.

"You say they don't want to learn," Dr. Monett repeated.

"I've tried so hard to be a good teacher. Tried and tried."

The lines in his face deepened and his hazel eyes, maybe because my voice was too shrill or I had spoken too many trieds, took on a compassionate dimension.

"I finally gave up my lectures. No one ever listened anyway. Mr. Thompson, that's the principal, began observing me a lot, and, well...well... You've probably met Mr. Thompson."

"He says you're a very good teacher. You have—what did he call it—sensitivity?"

"If sensitivity is recognizing hopelessness, yes, I have it." I was talking too quickly again, too emotionally. I deliberately slowed the pace of my words. "The truth is I am a good teacher."

Dr. Monett looked genuinely skeptical.

"I want the very best for my students. So many, many of them have disappointed me, failed me."

"So many of them have failed you," Dr. Monett repeated.

I did not like the way he kept repeating everything I said, a method he had secured, no doubt, from some absurd book. "It all has to do with..." I was going to say meeting responsibility, but I didn't want to sound like my wife. "It doesn't matter. I don't have to work, anyway."

"You say you don't have to work."

This constant repetition destroyed my ability to place any confidence in him. "My wife. You know Marjorie?"

"Yes." He straightened up, interested, now. "I've read her articles. A very fine writer."

"She makes all the money. I suppose you want me to talk about her."

"Would you like to talk about Marjorie?"

Anxiety flooded between us again. I couldn't answer him from the roar of it.

The books behind him began talking through his thin, serious lips. He tried every approach, but I was able to construct no answers. I could not even move my eyes from his face. He talked on and on until at last, exhausted, he paused long enough for me to rise to my feet.

Dr. Monett stood up with me, a false little smile at the corners of his mouth. His eyes avoided mine, pretended not to notice the sweat that ran in little streams down my forehead. "Tomorrow," he said, "let's talk tomorrow."

The first words I had uttered in a very long time had left me shaken and desperate. I had made wonderful progress, or had I? Had I, instead, reaffirmed all that Marjorie had told him?

With panic I heard the door to the ward click shut behind me. I should have had out-patient treatment or at least a private room. But Marjorie, because I refused to speak a word to her or because she always made all the decisions, actually suggested this.

But I didn't belong here.

Three of my ward-mates stood near the TV, but nobody watched it. I crossed to my bunk, lay down, and tried to shut everything out. The pressure I had felt in the doctor's office increased until it physically immobilized me.

I could hear the man I liked the least, the huge, gray-haired man, mumbling to himself. He carried a blank sheet of paper with him everywhere he went. Now he waved the paper, shouting, "Good work, isn't it?"

Although I didn't open my eyes, I realized with dread he was standing over me. "Damn good job, huh?"

I could feel the sheet of paper smack my face. I brought my hand up defensively.

"What do you think?"

Wearily I lifted myself up on my elbow and examined the blank paper. He was a lunatic. His success was all make-believe.

He began waving the paper frantically, his eyes growing more and more irrational. "No one else would have thought of it. It's a good idea, isn't it?"

I drew on all my past experience as a teacher and finally verbalized the words he must hear, "Yes, very good work." I fell back on my bunk with eyes tightly shut.

"If it weren't for you," he said confidentially, "I'd quit. No one here deserves this kind of work. What's your name?"

"Smith," I said.

"Well, Smith, I like you. I'll see to it you get a promotion."

Already I dreaded my next meeting with Dr. Monett. I pleaded to God for the strength to go into his office and actually talk about my wife. As the time drew closer, I had no force for the task. "I can't see Dr. Monett today." It was a struggle to speak but desperation drove the words out of my throat.

In spite of my protests, the attendant took my arm and led me to the doctor's office.

"It's like taking a sledge hammer, chopping, grinding a rock into powder. It takes time, sweat, effort. Then Marjorie says, 'Put that rock back together again!' You can't imagine how worthless, how helpless... Then she yells, 'You never could take any responsibility!'"

Dr. Monett, so very quiet today, listened with an index finger under his heavy chin.

"And my daughter. Sandy. She's a...a slut. I had to watch Marjorie ruin her. Marjorie can do it; she can ruin anyone. She gets worse every year."

"Marjorie or Sandy?"

"Both of them. Worse every year." I had begun to ramble, begun to sweat. "Then Marjorie says, `She's your daughter. Why can't you straighten her out? Why don't you ever take any responsibility?'"

"You didn't have any part in...ruining your daughter, as you put it?"

His hazel eyes, wary, had narrowed in accusation. It was obvious what he thought. "I...no. No, I had no part in it. I'm not even a little guilty. I read Wordsworth to her. And Emerson! Does that sound like I was trying to ruin her? And I followed her into bars and dope dens. And time and again I even called the police to protect her. You don't understand. I've done everything I can to see that she's had every chance."

The chair squeaked as the big man turned a little and settled back into it. "Sometimes the truth is a dragon," he said slowly, as if talking to a six-year-old. "No one wants to face a dragon, now do they? So, we cower. We make excuses. It's entirely human. Nothing to be defensive about. Nothing to be frightened of."

"This is not my dragon! I had no part in Sandy's destruction. I did everything to help her! I am not guilty!" My voice had grown very high, very loud. "Not guilty! Not responsible!"

Dr. Monett quickly pressed a button on his desk. "Take Mr. Smith back to his room," he said.

* * *

After that I refused to keep my appointments with Dr. Monett. They tried pleading with me, leading me to his office, but I held my ground. I had no idea what trouble it would cause me.

Often the doctor would come into my room, sit by my bunk, and chat pleasantly about the election, the weather, his family. I would lay with my arm across my face so I would not have to see him.

One such day after a lengthy discourse about his roots, he inquired about my early years. Something about what he had been saying made me think of Beth.

"My sister," I said.

"Your sister?"

"She's been dead for only six months. It was horrible, the way she died. So slowly, so terribly. She was the only one I could really talk to. Do you know what I mean?"

"You could talk to her."

"Yes. I could talk to her. The only one."

Sad, hazel eyes, filling with pity, urged me to continue.

"It's awful, isn't it, to lose the ones you can't bear to lose and have all the others around, the ones you can't talk to."

"I think your sister would want you to talk to me."

I said nothing.

"About your life. About Marjorie."

"No! No! Please go away!"

Marjorie and Dr. Monett had been conferring often; I could tell by the way they glanced at each other whenever I said or did anything in their presence. I heard him tell her, "Patience is what we must have. Even though he has refused to come into my office, I feel we are making progress. The very best thing for him now is a visit home."

"Sandy is expecting us in twenty minutes," Marjorie said as she came toward my bunk.

"I'd rather not go."

"What nonsense. It will do you good." Dr. Monett and she exchanged looks.

"No," I said weakly.

"Now you get right up, Everett. We don't want to be late."

No one would believe that Marjorie, so small, so delicately groomed, would be capable of ugly manipulations, twisted dominations. In the end she coerced me into following her from the sprawling, brick building, although I stared straight ahead and stolidly denied her any answers to her flood of hateful questions.

The drive to Sandy's I dreaded most of all. I felt I could endure her talk, even seeing Sandy, but Marjorie's driving—I braced one hand tightly against the dash.

When the first car tried to pass us, Marjorie stepped on the gas. For a while we cruised neck to neck, then with growing determination, Marjorie gained and pulled ahead. The other driver honked his horn in irritation as he fell back. Marjorie smiled and I felt myself quaking. Why didn't she ever ease off? Other people had goals, too. Would it hurt to let a few of them go by?

I had improved enough under Dr. Monett's care to take a stand. "Marjorie," I said, "Why don't you not talk to Sandy about certain things."

"Good God, Everett, she knows all about you. It's just that Sandy wouldn't think of going to that place to see you."

"That's not what I mean. Please, Marjorie, please don't talk about Larry."

Larry, a rather ambitionless youth, a nice boy, had asked Sandy to marry him. The marriage loomed as Sandy's one chance to straighten up her life. If only Marjorie would let it happen.

"You expect me to pretend that he's acceptable? That's your solution to everything, isn't it? Pretend."

"No. The truth is I see everything very clearly."

She brought a thin hand up to her forehead. "Sure you do," she said with exasperation.

"Don't discuss Larry today, Marjorie. For my sake."

Marjorie made a hissing noise through white, even teeth. I let go of the dash and leaned back, my eyes closed. Another car must have attempted to pass. I felt the automobile shoot forward, careen in and out, felt it brake and stop on a dime. "Damn fool," Marjorie said. "He almost caused us to wreck."

"Larry's coming over at five," Sandy announced as we walked into the small house. She looked particularly bad today, hair frizzed so it all but stood straight up, thick green splotches of color all around her eyes.

"Good, that will give me a chance to talk to him," Marjorie said. She nodded her head to me. "He should be back at four. I'll let you take him back, and I'll cook up a little supper for Larry, you and me."

Sandy shrugged. "Hey, I'm going to be gone for a while. You both just hang around, OK?" Having never so much as glanced at me, Sandy walked out the door.

"I'm going to catch my program," Marjorie said, switching on the TV. "You go out and check the car. No one's even looked at it since you left. It's your responsibility to keep it running."

I pulled Marjorie's Ford into the attached garage and lifted the hood. My head was spinning. I could hardly depend on my eyes to read the markings on the oil stick. My hands began shaking more and more as I continued to do things to the car. A churning had started in my brain, a churning I could hear. I worked frantically faster and faster, no longer paying any attention to what I was doing. I drained out most of the brake fluid; most all of the fluids that gave the car life; I loosened one back wheel so it barely remained attached. I...I don't even know what all I did, but finally I stopped, walked back into the house, washed the grease off my hands.

Sandy's little Toyota soon pulled to a screeching stop in front of the house. Sandy breezed inside. "You want to go, Pop? It's almost four."

"We haven't even...I mean, you and I didn't even get a chance to say..."

Sandy shrugged.

Marjorie looked up from the TV. "You talk to Dr. Monett, now."

We were half-way back to Reimer's before I attempted to communicate with Sandy. "About Larry," I began. "Don't let Marjorie..."

"Mum's right about him, I'm afraid," she said. "He's never going to take any responsibility."

Later that evening, I was led into Dr. Monett's office. He was waiting for me at the door, his heavy face a mask of tragedy. Through the layers and layers of anxiety, I could barely see him.

"I hate to be the one to tell you, Everett."

Awful silence gripped my throat like a hand.

Dr. Monett guided me to the chair I usually sat in and stood over me, his fingers reluctant to loose my arm. "It's your wife. It's Marjorie. She's been in an accident."

I shook my head. My hands went to my face.

"She's dead, Everett. She was passing a car and they hit head-on. She died instantly. It's comforting, Everett, to know that she didn't suffer any."

I looked up at him, tears running unchecked down my face. "I killed her!" The words came out in a gasp.

He loosed my arm, patted my shoulder, and moved backward to lean against his desk.

"I tampered with the car! I did everything to it I could! Her death is my fault! My fault!"

Dr. Monett frowned. I had become accustomed to that expression of correction, of non-verbal disagreement. How could I convince him that I was telling the truth?

"Mr. Smith. Your wife had an accident. You are in no way responsible."

"I am!" I stood up, sweat running down my face, down my armpits. "You've got to believe me. I meddled with everything on the car. Everything. I wanted to hurt her. I wanted to stop her once and for all. Why do you refuse to understand? I killed her. I'm guilty. Guilty!"

The doctor's eyes avoided mine. "It is common for patients like you to become depressed. This condition generally causes a distortion in the way happenings are viewed. This guilt you feel is simply your way of trying to feel in charge again. It will pass. Believe me."

My voice had a frantic pitch. I tried hard to control it. "You must believe me. I am responsible. Me! I'm responsible!"

The Secret Admirer
By Vickie Britton

Is Amanda's secret admirer the man of her dreams, or her worst nightmare?

Amanda passed the laundry and walked into the small room next to it that housed the post office boxes for the huge Flagstone Apartments. It was bare and deserted. Amanda unlocked her box and drew out a single item of mail. She studied the unfamiliar handwriting curiously. No return. Only her name and address scrawled in flowing script across the front of the envelope.

Frowning, Amanda hastened to unfold an ordinary sheet of typing paper. "To Amanda, my true love." Her gaze dropped to the signature at the bottom, "Your Secret Admirer."

Amanda's heart soared as she immediately thought of Sean Myers, the new man at the insurance office where she worked. Although sending an anonymous love letter seemed out of character for the soft-spoken, reserved young executive, she could not mistake the fact that he had been paying special attention to her lately.

Intrigued by the mystery, Amanda barely noticed the tall, thin man who had just entered the room. He seemed to purposefully brush past Amanda on his way to the row of boxes in the far corner, but he did not apologize or even glance toward her.

Surely, the letter must be from Sean, Amanda concluded with a smile. A vision of his earnest blue eyes and sandy blond hair formed in her mind as she tucked the note back into the envelope.

Paying more attention to her private thoughts than to what she was doing, Amanda unexpectedly collided with the man who had entered and who had by now collected his mail. She gave a startled cry as the envelope slipped from her hands and fluttered to the floor near his feet. He reached down to retrieve the letter for her, then gallantly handed it back, saying, "Apartment number sixty-five. That makes us neighbors."

Amanda was certain she had never before seen this man around the complex. She would have noticed him, thin to a point of gauntness, with longish, rust-colored hair and piercing dark eyes. Feeling uneasy, she murmured a quick thank you, and hurried away, ducking into the dark stairwell that led up to her third-floor apartment.

Later, a cup of steaming tea before her, Amanda lingered over the letter. The only other man who might have written this was that smart-aleck manager of Flagstone Apartments, Wiley Freeman. She brushed that notion aside quickly: the love note simply had to be from Sean.

The next morning at work, Amanda found herself watching Sean closely. His earnest blue eyes gave away no secrets. The minute he disappeared into his office down the hall, Amanda cornered her friend Peggy near the coffee urn, eager to seek her opinion. "Peg, what do you make of this?"

Serious gray eyes behind thick spectacles scanned the amorous message, then focused on Amanda. "So you have an admirer." Her voice was edged with sharpness, almost as if she were envious.

Amanda, lowering the volume of her voice, asked, "Do you think Sean might have sent it?"

The jangle of bracelets announced the approach of Lynette, who worked with Sean in the adjacent office. She drifted up behind them in a cloud of Georgio perfume and poured herself a cup of coffee. "So what's the latest?"

"Amanda's got a secret admirer," Peggy replied.

Thrilled, Lynette read over Peggy's shoulder. "Romantic!" she exclaimed. "We'll have to find out who this mystery lover is."

"How will we do that?" Peg inquired.

Lynette placed her hands on her hips. "Leave it to me. I'll be your sleuth. Clues, anyone?"

"She suspects it might be Sean."

Lynette hooted. "She wishes! The Brad Pitt of the office? I don't think so, but there's one way to find out for sure."

Amanda was wishing she hadn't told anyone.

"How?" Peggy was saying, excitedly now.

"I'll just up and snitch a sample of his handwriting, and we'll do our own analysis. If the loops and swirls match...then we'll have him. Get back to you later."

Amanda found she could not concentrate on her work. She watched the hands of the clock move, making their wretchedly slow circle. Lynette, who must not have succeeded in her mission, still had not reported back by the time the hour reached five.

Amanda, feeling let down and disappointed, started her long walk home. She shivered a little. On days like this she wished she owned a car. The cold had grown bitter, the dark wind hinted of snow.

She hadn't gone far when she heard a horn beep directly beside her.

Nervously Amanda glanced around, then smiled as Sean called, "Want a lift?"

She slipped in beside him, and the two of them made polite conversation about the chilly wind and how quickly the days were darkening. As the small, cozy Chinese restaurant on the corner, where Amanda often dined alone, came into view, Sean suggested, "How about dinner?"

They entered, walking between statues of giant red dragons, into a room dark and intimate. As they shared a platter of appetizers, Sean confided shyly, "I've been looking for an excuse to take you out for months now. I'm just not too comfortable about meeting...people."

"I'm glad you asked me." Amanda took another butterfly shrimp from the platter. "I sometimes dread eating alone."

"The city can be a lonely place," Sean agreed.

Amanda gazed into his sincere blue eyes. She liked the rugged look of him, the easy smile, the way his sandy hair spilled boyishly across his forehead.

Amanda and Sean talked effortlessly over main courses then lingered over tea and fortune cookies. Amanda felt as if she had known him for years. Even though Sean made no mention of the letter, Amanda was overjoyed by the knowledge that he was the sender.

"Do you know that man?" Sean asked.

Amanda glanced across the deep red interior of the restaurant. When she saw the thin, red-headed man she had met in the post office yesterday, she drew in a sharp breath.

His dark, probing eyes bored into hers. She looked away quickly, telling Sean, "He's my neighbor. He lives at the Flagstone Apartments."

Sean frowned. "I don't like the way he keeps staring at you. How well do you know him?"

"We've barely spoken."

"Keep it that way," Sean said, reaching across the table for her hand.

They were so close to the apartment that they walked rather than drove. Ever since he had mentioned the red-haired man in the restaurant, Sean had seemed preoccupied. Now this emotion deepened into worry. "This stairwell could be dangerous, especially at night. A mugger could pull a gun or knife on you before you even realize what is happening. I used to live here, when I first moved to town last year. Is Wiley Freeman still the manager?"

She thought of the wise-cracking, smug-faced apartment manager. "Yes, and you know what kind of response I get from him when I complain about anything."

"Then I'll do the complaining for you." Sean lingered a moment outside her door. "I'll be out of town for the next few days. But how about a real date, say next Friday night?"

"That would be wonderful."

"I'll come by for you at eight, then."

Now that Amanda knew who her secret admirer was, she wished Lynette would simply forget about playing sleuth.

"See?" Lynette cried triumphantly Monday morning. "The handwriting matches perfectly!" Peggy and Lynette had gotten into her desk drawer and were comparing Amanda's anonymous love letter with some papers snitched from Sean's office. "Same loops on the *L*, same large, black dot on the *I*."

Lynette saw immediately what Amanda already knew. The two writing samples had doubtlessly been penned by the same hand. Sean was, indeed, her "secret admirer."

"I just knew it was him!"

"We have a date this Friday night."

"Romantic!" Lynette cried.

"Wish it was me," Peggy added.

Friday. Five days seemed such a long time to wait, so many evenings to spend all alone. After settling into her room that evening, Amanda was startled by a sharp rapping on the door. "Sean?" she called out. His name came immediately to mind even though she knew he had doubtlessly left for his business trip.

"No, it's not Sean," a familiar voice mimicked.

Amanda opened the door to Wiley Freeman's perpetually smirking face. In his arms were a dozen red roses.

"What is this?"

"S-p-e-c-i-a-l D-e-l-i-v-e-r-y. " He shrugged his shoulders beneath the sloppy gray sweatshirt. "I found these sitting outside my office door." Mockingly, he read the attached note, "To Amanda, my obsession. Until Friday. Your Secret Admirer." Small, gray eyes challenged hers. "Tell Lover Boy we're not running a parcel service around here, OK? If it doesn't fit in the box downstairs, tell him to send it U.P.S. I can't spend my life running up and down these stairs."

"You know you need the exercise, Wiley," Amanda countered. "And, by the way, why don't you fix some lights on that stairwell before someone falls and breaks their neck?"

Wiley gave a derisive laugh. "Have to work on that after hours. My days are scheduled full."

Amanda closed the door between them and hurried to find a vase for the lovely red roses.

Wednesday evening after work, Amanda found a small parcel in her box. Another gift from Sean? She was on her way back to her apartment when the red-haired man with the intense eyes confronted her by the dark, empty laundry. "Amanda. I must talk to you."

Fear made her voice shake. "What do you want?"

"Did you know there was a murder here last year, right in this apartment building? A young woman, about your age..."

He grasped her arm as she started to back away.

His strange dark eyes glittered. "I must warn you. That man you were with in the restaurant, I know something about him. You must listen."

Amanda freed her arm and ducked into the stairwell, relieved to find Wiley Freeman tinkering with the electricity. Wiley looked up from his work, his small eyes bright in his pimply face. "Your Lover Boy called and insisted I fix the lights. But I don't know what's wrong here. Better go back and study my manuals."

"Wiley, do you know that man?" Amanda asked anxiously.

"What man?" Wiley turned, but the red-haired stranger had vanished like a ghost.

"The tall man with red hair. He says he lives here."

Wiley frowned. "I don't have any red-headed tenants."

"He keeps trying to frighten me." Amanda paused. "He told me there was a murder in this apartment building last year. Is that true?"

"Naw." Wiley turned back to his work so she could not see his face. "Not that I'd tell anyone if there was. I'd just haul out the corpse, wipe up the blood, and put the old For Rent sign back on the door."

"That sounds just like you."

"What's that you're holding?" Wiley asked, his gaze locking on the parcel in her hand. "Another gift from Lover Boy?"

Amanda attempted to return his joking tone. "Is that any of your business?"

Wiley's eyes rolled upward. "And to think that I'm fixing these stairway lights just for you!"

Banter with Wiley took the edge off the anxiety she felt concerning the red-haired stranger. If there had been a murder here, Wiley would have told her. Why had that man been trying to frighten her like that?

No longer even wanting to open the package, Amanda reluctantly undid the outside wrappings. Beneath a layer of white tissue, she found a filmy, very sexy, black negligee.

The gift made her feel embarrassed, a little insulted. Would Sean really send her such an intimate gift when they had just met? Her gaze fell to the enclosed note. "To Amanda—my desire. Your Secret Admirer."

Amanda frowned. This didn't seem like Sean at all. Yet, who else could be the sender? A vision of the red-haired stranger caused a chill to creep up her spine. Were the letter, flowers, and gift from him? He could easily have gotten her name and address from the envelope the day she had dropped her letter in the mail room. But how could he possibly imitate Sean's exact style of writing?

Amanda once more compared the new note with the one accompanying the flowers, then with the copy taken from Sean's desk. The distinct, flowing handwriting, identical on each paper, proclaimed the same person had written each note.

The telephone rang out shrilly, startling her. Amanda's heart chilled as she listened to eerie, rasping breathing on the other end of the line.

"Who is this?" she demanded.

"This is your secret admirer. Did you get my gift?"

The voice sounded muffled and disguised. "I can't wait until Friday night. I can't wait to see you all dressed up for me in that sexy black lace...."

Amanda, heart pounding, flung down the receiver.

When the phone rang again, at first Amanda refused to answer. Finally, gathering courage, she answered. "Hello."

"Amanda. Sean."

How could he sound so calm, so normal? "This isn't funny, Sean."

"I'm not actually trying to be funny. What do you mean?"

"I don't know what kind of demented thrill you're getting out of this, but I want you to know, our date is off. In fact, I never want to see you again."

Amanda hung up. The phone rang over and over again. She listened, immobile, tears stinging her eyes.

Amanda tensed at the sight of the solitary letter in her box Thursday evening. With trembling fingers she opened it. On the plain white paper two words were scrawled, "Until Friday."

A surge of panic filled her. This sick joke of Sean's had gone far enough. Why wouldn't he leave her alone? Amanda thought of the red-haired man's warnings and about how little she knew about Sean, not even where he had come from before he had drifted into Kansas City.

Amanda considered taking the note to the police. But how could she when it had no signature? Until Friday—those words certainly carried no threat by themselves. Then why did she feel so intimidated, so terrified by the portent of their veiled meaning?

As Amanda started up to her apartment, she thought she saw someone standing near the base of the stairwell, someone who slipped away like a cat between the high, towering walls of the apartment building.

She hurried to flip one of the two switches that Wiley had installed at the top and base of the stairwell. Nothing but darkness. Was he ever going to connect those lights?

Her anger at Wiley was soon replaced by an eerie suspicion of him. Wiley had delivered the roses, had read the note to her that said Until Friday.

She thought of the ugly phone call, the tasteless black lingerie that looked as if it had come straight out of one of his girlie magazines. Could Wiley have copied Sean's handwriting on the note that he had delivered to her room? Was Wiley, not Sean, the person she should fear?

A terrible sense of dread filled Amanda as five o'clock Friday approached. Terrified of being alone, she caught up with Peggy in the hallway and suggested that they have dinner together.

"But aren't you meeting Sean tonight?" she asked. "I know he wasn't at work today, but won't he be back from his trip in time for your date?"

"The date's been canceled."

Peggy stared at Amanda through the lenses of her glasses as if she had lost her mind. "If someone that handsome would ask me out..." she started, but the words faded away.

Over dinner, Amanda thought about confiding in Peg, about telling her about the frightening phone call. Instead, she asked, "What do you actually know about Sean?"

Peggy shrugged. "Nothing much. He's a little stand-offish with everyone, hard to get acquainted with. But I do know he's cute and that he's simply crazy about you."

"How do you know that?"

Peg's eyes seemed to glitter strangely. "I knew right from the start Sean was your secret admirer. He wanted everything to be perfect for you. In fact," she confessed, "I'm the one who helped him pick out the card and order those lovely roses."

* * *

The huge old apartment building loomed dark and frightening. Still fearful of being alone, Amanda lingered at the library where Peggy had dropped her off. When the building closed at a nine o'clock, she reluctantly started toward home.

If Sean had dared to show up for their date, he would be long gone by now.

During the quiet, deserted walk, apprehension stole over her. She kept glancing over her shoulder, interpreting every slight noise as the stealthy step of some stalker.

She should have confided her fears to Peggy and asked if she could spend the night at her house, but it was too late for that now.

Amanda paused at the base of the stairs and looked back. Had she actually heard footsteps this time? Her gaze roamed through the dark tree branches, attempting to pierce the black spaces not illuminated by the faint glow of streetlight.

She must hurry up to her room. Once there she would feel safe behind the bolted door. Before she entered the dark stairway, she caught a glimpse of a form far behind her.

Amanda began to race up the steps to her room. Somehow she instinctively knew where to step in the utter blackness.

She reached the darkest part of the stairwell, the small landing leading to the second floor. The steps to the third floor rose just above her. At that moment Amanda became aware that she was not alone.

She could not make out the features of the waiting man. He existed only as a monstrous black shadow. She screamed once, before angry hands caught her, one of them clamping around her mouth. The fingers of the other hand coiled around her wind-pipe, blocking off her very breath.

Amanda fought desperately to break the brutal grip. She managed to free herself, falling down hard on the small, wooden landing. Bright stars danced in front of her eyes, then vanished slowly into a deep, horrid blackness.

Even though she saw nothing, she was bombarded by sounds. Heavy footsteps ran past her, very near the spot where she lay. She heard the sound of blows. Then a harsh cry arose, resounding against the narrow walls around her.

Amanda tried to rise, to move away from the form that had whirled and taken flight. She could not get out of the way in time. His feet stumbled against her, and the unexpected collision sent him hurling down the steps toward the first floor.

"Hey, what's going on down there?"

Blinding light flooded the stairwell. At the top of the stairs, at the landing that led to her floor, hand on the light switch, stood Wiley Freeman.

Sean, his eyes remaining on Amanda, did not answer, just started down the stairs toward her. His clothes were ruffled and torn and there was blood running down his jaw across his shirt.

Amanda glanced in terror behind her. At the bottom of the stairs sprawled the unconscious form of the red-haired man.

Sean gently helped her to her feet. "He was waiting for me," Amanda sobbed, "hiding in the darkness."

"It's all right. It's all over now." Sean gathered her in his arms and held her close.

"When I couldn't find you, I called Peg. She told me she had let you off at the library. I followed you from there." He drew her close against him. "I'm so glad I did!"

Wiley used his cellular phone to summon the police and soon two officers arrived to handcuff the intruder.

"We've questioned this man before," the older policeman said, "when that girl disappeared from this apartment complex last month."

"He must have spotted me in this building while he was stalking her," Amanda said. "Later he got my name and number when he picked up the envelope I dropped at the mail room."

After the three of them watched the red-haired man, still dazed, being led to the waiting police car, Amanda told Sean about the black negligee, the frightening phone call. "I should have known it wasn't you. But how could he have known we had a date tonight? How could he have copied your handwriting?"

"The roses sat downstairs outside my office a long time before I brought them up," Wiley confessed. "He must have traced a portion of the note so he could mimic Sean's handwriting."

"I've learned my lesson," Sean said, holding Amanda close. "Next time I want to say I love you, I'll say it in person. No more anonymous letters." He sealed his promise with a short, tender kiss.

Wiley Freeman gave a resigned, good-natured grin. "Hey," he said to Amanda, "instead of kissing him, you should be thanking me for fixing the lights."

Amanda laughed. "Believe me I'm glad I'm no longer in the dark, especially about my secret admirer."

The Muse Incarnate
By Vickie Britton

*When Roan steals Darien Port's girlfriend, he finds he is doing
the man an immortal favor.*

"A man could certainly live a life of quiet desperation
out here," Roan Gage said to himself as he watched
the mallards dip and glide into the silvery strip of
water in back of the cottage. He was beginning to feel a kinship
with Thoreau. The New England scene before him could have
been right out of Walden Pond.

April's parents had offered him the use of the cottage for the
summer even though they thought he was ruining their only
daughter's life. He supposed he should be grateful.

The ducks seemed oblivious to the morning chill. Roan shivered
a little, wishing he had thrown a sweater over the thin T-shirt. Keeping
a steady pace, he began to jog around the lake. He ignored the
throbbing ache in his legs, the icy stabs of air invading his lungs.
Physical exertion was his personal way of courting the Muse.

Roan Gage. Thirty-five years old. The heavy pounding of his
feet could not drown out the anxious thoughts that circled like
vultures in his brain. Roan Gage. Failure.

For Roan, the torch of fame had burned briefly, then fizzled out with the rise and fall of his one and only successful novel, *A Time of Reckoning*. Since then, he had barely supported himself by ghosting for several famous authors. This summer was his big chance to make a comeback. The cabin provided the isolation he needed. He had promised April and his agent that he would have the new manuscript completed by summer's end.

Roan circled the pond once more, following the worn path made by his restless footsteps. He continued to jog, ignoring the dampness that made the cotton T-shirt now cling clammily to his skin, the aching pressure deep in his lungs. He did not stop until the runner's high burst forth from the core of his being, filling his limbs with boundless energy, making a kaleidoscope of thoughts race dizzily through his mind.

And then the miracle occurred. A vision. The wonderful workings of the Muse never failed to amaze him.

Breathless, Roan stumbled the last few yards to the cottage, anxious to tame the windfall of errant thoughts, to get them down on paper before they vanished into the thin morning air.

Before he could get to the computer, the telephone rang. At first, the noise startled him. He hadn't even been sure the line still worked after last week's storm.

Roan searched the pile of books and clutter upon the desk, freeing the cord from the tangle of debris. He lifted the receiver to his ear, expecting his fiancé, April, to answer. "Hello?"

Through the rattle of static came a wispy woman's voice that carried a foreign, exotic lilt. Definitely not the voice of April. "Roan? Roan Gage?"

"Speaking." He tried to create some visual image of the speaker, but the bad connection gave the voice an ageless, formless quality as if it belonged to some disembodied spirit.

"Sorry to disturb you, Mr. Gage. I got your number from your agent." Roan frowned. Wealthy widows, the wives of deceased actors and politicians, often sought him out, eager for someone to write their memoirs. Roan's agent knew he was in seclusion; he had asked him to filter all calls.

"I am Leisha, Darien Port's personal secretary."

"Darien Port—" Roan caught his breath at the sound of the name. Darien was one of the most powerful writers on the East Coast.

"Mr. Port would like to know if you would stop by some evening. Of course, your agent explained that you may wish to decline."

"Decline?" Ignore an invitation from Darien Port? Roan thought he would be as likely to dismiss a summons from the White House. "On the contrary, I'd be honored!"

"Perfect!" The voice on the other end of the line seemed to lift, lighten, or maybe the static had cleared. Laughter followed; airy, beguiling, like the whisper of wind chimes through a gentle breeze.

Roan formed his first mental picture of the speaker on the telephone and the vision made him feel weak in the knees. The exotic lilt of her voice hinted of exquisite beauty, of long-lashed green eyes and lengths of flowing black hair. Such is the stuff fantasy is made of, he sighed. He almost didn't hear her next words, "We have drinks around eight. May we expect you then?"

"Tonight?"

"Darien says there's no time like the present. We're really quite close, you know. The big, stone house on the left. The only other house out here, so you really can't miss it."

Roan lingered for a moment after the connection was broken, cradling the receiver in his hand. Could one fall in love with a voice? Even as Roan scoffed at the idea, his betraying heart fluttered like a trapped bird against the fetters of his rib cage.

Roan sat down at the computer, but all of the ideas he could hardly wait to put on paper had spilled through his mind like sand through an upturned hourglass.

The old man must want a ghost. That was the only reason a famous name like Darien Port would contact a virtual unknown. Roan had ghosted for several prominent authors in the old man's circle, but never for the great Darien Port. Everyone knew that Darien Port's work was original.

So why would he all of a sudden want a ghostwriter? It didn't matter. Whatever the reason, Roan simply wasn't for hire. He had spent too many years fattening the purse and reputation of others. This summer was his alone.

As he rummaged through the closet, Roan cursed himself for accepting the invitation. His search produced a good, though slightly crumpled jacket, seriously dated by corduroy patches upon the elbows. Since he hadn't had the good sense to turn the invitation down, he would do the next best thing...have a few drinks at Darien Port's expense, maybe flirt a little with the woman whose voice on the phone had taken his breath away.

A vision of Leisha, as he imagined her to be, materialized in his mind once more. A lucid image, one so clear he could see the delicate curve of her cheek, the vivid green of her eyes. What did she really look like, the woman with such captivating voice? With the entire field of his imagination at play, why did this particular image stick in the mind? He usually preferred tall, athletic blondes like April.

The day passed uneventfully. Impatiently, Roan glanced at the clock, wondering if the hands would ever move. But it was no longer world-famous author Darien Port that Roan was anxious to meet. It was Leisha...Leisha...Leisha.

Reality usually let Roan Gage down. He had chosen to become a writer in the first place in order to create his own world, to counter his many disappointments when his dreams fell short of perfection. But not this time.

Startled by the accuracy of his own imagination, Roan stared from the huge country house with its tall spires and thick stone walls to the woman who stood waiting for him at the doorway. He felt as if he'd entered a dream.

The vision with flowing hair dressed in lengths of pale silk could have been created solely from the image in his own mind. Her long-lashed emerald eyes held his entranced, as her full red lips parted in an enigmatic smile. The effect rendered him speechless.

Roan wondered if she had also conjured up an image of him and was vain enough to hope that his windswept, unruly hair and lean-muscled body did justice to that image.

"Welcome, Roan Gage," she said finally, and did not look disappointed. Her voice, soft and yet husky, held that same aura of mystery for him as it had over the telephone line. As she reached toward him with a pale hand, drawing him toward the entrance, he felt the pressure of her fingers, surprisingly strong, on his wrist. The pale, unpolished nails nipped lightly at his skin. She seemed so much more wraith than flesh and blood that he was grateful for the slight sensation of pain, which assured him she was not a figment of his imagination.

He followed her into the house, watching the way the dark curtain of hair cascaded to the small of her back. Her step was light and airy, as alluring as any siren's song.

Darien Port waited in a high, wing-backed chair that matched the rest of the dimly-lit parlor's decor. He wore a dark smoking jacket and about his neck a jeweled cravat. "So glad you could accept my invitation, Mr. Gage. Pardon me for not rising to greet you." With a gesture, he indicated the silver-tipped cane propped near his chair.

Time had worn away at the edges, but had not quite eroded the last vestiges of grandeur from Darien's weathered face. The man's wealth and power were reinforced by the dark opulence of the room, the heavy, wooden furniture, the weighed velvet drapes.

"I have read all of your works, Mr. Port," Roan said, taking the heavy-ringed hand that was offered him.

Darien inclined his white head graciously. "And I in turn was quite impressed with your book, *A Time of Reckoning.*"

Roan allowed himself an embarrassed glow of pleasure. Few had read his one and only accomplishment, which had all too soon plunged into the abyss of oblivion.

"I'll get the wine." Leisha spoke at their side. "White or red, Darling?"

The personal way Leisha addressed her employer surprised Roan, then filled him with keen disappointment. Was Leisha more than a secretary to Mr. Port, more than a live-in companion? Despite the vast differences in their ages—Mr. Port was old enough to be the girl's father—were they lovers?

"Whatever our guest prefers," Darien responded, barely affording her a glance.

The intense way Leisha turned her gaze upon Roan, waiting for his answer as if it were the most important thing in the world to her, made him uneasy. She was so beautiful he had to force himself not to stare. Brows, thick and dark, made a natural frame for her cut-emerald eyes, fathomless eyes that focused solely upon him. Eyes filled with some ethereal sorrow.

He wanted suddenly to hold her in his arms, to kiss that sorrow away. Instead, he forced himself to look down, away from her, battling desire. "Red," he managed to murmur.

She gave a throaty laugh of approval. "I always preferred that, too."

Roan glanced up again, into the depths of those green eyes, cat's eyes, the pupils huge and elongated. How could she, a total stranger, fill him with such intense longing? She licked her lips, the scarlet mouth parting into a secret smile. Roan caught his breath as she disappeared into the adjoining room. Few words had passed between them. But the unspoken message in her eyes, the silent language of woman to man, was undeniable. She wanted him.

Guiltily, Roan turned his attention back to his host. Darien Port's face was gray, ashen, unsmiling, the heavy brow furrowed as if by some long-suffered pain. Roan felt a tense moment, knowing Darien could not have missed his open admiration for the woman who called the old man endearments, who was most likely an intimate companion.

"Is my Leisha not the picture of the ideal woman?" Darien Port commented unexpectedly.

"Beautiful," Roan agreed quietly. "The Muse Incarnate."

"I found her on an island. A primitive, isolated place." Darien spoke as if he had almost forgotten Roan's presence. "She wanted to see the world. I had the money, the means to give her opportunity, so I took her with me. I taught her to read." Darien's voice broke suddenly. "An unholy mistake."

Before Roan could ponder his words, the old man said with a wave of his hand, "But enough about her." A brightness glowed like a fever in his pale blue eyes as they fastened themselves upon Roan. "You've probably guessed that I've invited you here for more than a social call," he said bluntly. And Roan was reassured that something more important occupied Mr. Port's mind, something that made his social trespass pale to insignificance. True to Roan's prediction, Darien Port confided with a sense of desperation, "I need a ghost."

Words of protest formed on Roan's lips, but before he could voice them, Darien Port leaned forward in his chair. "Money is no object."

"It's not the money."

"Most men have a price," he persisted. He grasped his cane and with much difficulty rose and stepped over to the mahogany desk in the corner. He returned, his thick-knuckled hands clutching a box containing the incomplete manuscript.

Roan accepted it out of politeness, glanced at the sheaf of pages, then back at Darien Port, who watched him with rapt attention. "The manuscript must be completed by the end of August. My offer is one third of the royalties."

"One third—" Roan sucked in his breath. Such a generous offer. Roan weighed the manuscript in his hands against the one kicking in his mind like an unborn baby. His own book, even if it made the bestseller list, would only be worth a few hundred thousand at best. A book by the master, Darien Port, could gross royalties in the millions.

Roan felt torn. This was the summer of his own success. But the lure of financial abundance urged him to strangle his own neophyte idea at birth and accept the offer at once.

"I had planned to work on my own novel this summer." Roan stood his ground firmly, though the thought of promised wealth made his voice quiver.

"Then you must postpone your plans." Once more, an edge of desperation crept into the old man's voice. "This book must be finished."

Roan felt the thickness of the manuscript in progress, glanced at the page after page of painstakingly handwritten notes. "You have done so much already. Perhaps you should try to complete it yourself."

"If I could finish it myself, I wouldn't need a ghost."

"Is it because of the deadline?"

"The deadline...yes. But it's not only that." Darien brushed a hand across his thick, snow-white mane of hair. "I just can't seem to get the damned thing finished. The idea is always on my mind, haunting me, tormenting me. But the words won't come. Every time I think I have my thoughts together, they scatter like dust. And yet this book is an extension of my very soul." He finished in strangled voice, "If it is not completed, I fear I may die!"

Writer's block. Roan smiled a little at the irony of the situation. The bane of any author, the crippling disease that knew no distinction between master and novice, had toppled the ancient oak of Darien Port, or at least had brought him to his knees.

"I could try to find you someone else."

"No." His voice rose with insistence. "It has to be you."

"Why me?"

"Because you are young, talented, intelligent." As he spoke wooden words of praise, Roan saw that Darien's gaze had shifted beyond him, to Leisha, who had silently entered the room. He thought he heard Darien Port utter softly, almost to himself, "Because you've been chosen."

"What were you two talking about?" Leisha's eyes fastened upon the old man's face with a keen, devouring interest Roan secretly wished was for him.

As if extremely irritated by her intrusion, Darien rudely brushed away her curiosity with a sweep of his hand.

"What do two writers usually talk about when left to their own resources?" Roan quipped to break the tension.

"Then don't let me get in the way of your conversation," Leisha said modestly, extending to Darien a dark green bottle and shimmering corkscrew. Her gaze rested upon the old man's face, adoring, as if he were the wisest of sages. "I know all of Darien's little secrets, don't I, my Darling?"

Roan saw a gleam in Leisha's eyes as her gaze settled upon the sheath of papers he had placed upon the marble-topped end table. "Ah, the manuscript."

"Leave it alone!" Darien Port commanded. Roan noticed how Darien's fingers trembled as he struggled with the corkscrew. His unspoken resentment seemed as turbulent as the liquid that frothed and bubbled against the pressure of the cork. The stopper released with a sudden explosion. The bottle slipped from Darien's grasp and shattered upon the floor near his feet.

More disturbing than the seeping wine and broken glass was the look of pure rage on Darien's face as he glared at Leisha, his fingers still closed firmly around the jagged corkscrew.

A trick of light made Roan gasp a little. For a moment, it seemed Leisha's eyes had changed color. Moonlight from the window added flecks of silver to their murky depths, flecks that vanished as her emerald gaze met his head-on.

For the flash of an instant, he had caught a glimpse of another woman, quite different in manner and appearance, standing in her place. But, of course, that was impossible!

"I'll clean it up," Leisha offered, moving toward Darien.

"No!" Darien waved her away and sank heavily back into his chair. Roan noticed how his hands still trembled. "Just bring more wine."

As obedient as some Oriental Geisha, she quietly left the room. Once she was gone, Darien began to speak. "At first, I was everything to her. I thought she needed me, but too late—as is often the case—I realized it was the other way around."

Roan listened, politely averting his eyes from the pool of wine and broken glass upon the floor near their feet.

"It's hard for an old man like me to keep her happy." He gave a heavy sigh. "She grows restless."

"She seems so meek and gentle," Roan could not help but comment.

"She is a vampire," Darien responded with tortured eyes. A fist came down on the edge of his chair. "She sucks my blood!"

Roan felt a tiny shiver. He heard signs of madness in Darien Port's speech and saw unleashed violence in his eyes.

Before he could make a move toward the door, Leisha appeared, hovering at the entrance to the room, looking like a helpless waif. Roan felt a sudden reluctance to leave her there, a genuine fear for her safety.

"Darien? There's no more wine."

"In the cellar," he answered sharply.

Roan felt a renewed sense of outrage. Darien's treatment of this delicate beauty, as if he were the master and she a lowly slave girl, was appalling. What kind of a hold did the old man have on her?

Leisha's lips trembled. "You know I can't go down there alone."

"Damn you!" Darien reached for the stick that leaned against the side of his chair then sank back with a weary sigh. Turning to Roan, he said with an impatient gesture, "Go with her, then."

Roan followed Leisha through the dark, empty dining room, down stone steps and into a small, damp cellar. In the dim light, he could see wine racks lined against the wall.

"You choose."

Roan moved toward the rack and selected at random a bottle of Pinot Noir. As he mounted the stairs, he felt her voice pulling him back toward her.

"I am a prisoner here. Please help me."

Her words tore at his soul.

As he turned back, she drifted effortlessly into his arms. Her body felt so light, so weightless, she seemed more spirit than flesh and blood as she clung to him.

Roan felt giddy with desire as her lips teased his, brush-ing across his mouth and throat, leaving a trail of kisses. She nipped playfully at his neck, and he cried out at the sudden, unexpected sting of pain.

"I'm so sorry," she murmured. In a sort of trance, he gazed at her and her eyes seemed suddenly drained of all color until they were as black as her hair. He saw a drop of blood, his blood, gleaming upon sharp, little teeth that were white and slightly uneven. Slowly she licked her lips and the blood vanished into the red of her mouth.

"Take the manuscript," Leisha urged. "He'll send me to you, and then we can be alone."

His response was to press her against him in a lover's embrace, his lips joining hers as if to seal a promise.

"We must go back upstairs." Leisha's voice brought him back

to his senses. She was standing an arm's length from him, the bottle of Pinot Noir in her arms. He felt suddenly dizzy, intoxicated, as if he had already drunk the entire contents of the bottle of wine. Surely he had imagined it all: her plea, the kiss, the tiny drop of blood.

A brooding silence followed their return. Guilt seemed to permeate the atmosphere. Darien Port looked solemn, resigned, as if he somehow sensed that he had been conspired against.

They drank in silence. At length, Roan put down his glass, rose, and said awkwardly, "I really must be going now."

Leisha moved as if to follow Roan out, but was stopped by Darien's sharp words, an order. "Clean up the wine." He took up his silver-tipped stick. "I'll see our guest to the door."

Darien paused near the marble-topped table. As they reached the entrance to the house, Darien pressed the unfinished manuscript firmly into Roan's hands. "Take this with you."

Roan smiled faintly. "I admire your persistence."

"I'm an old man. I have persistence instead of time."

He felt the weight of the manuscript in his hand. "I'll return this to you, then, once I've made my decision."

"No need," Darien said. "I'll send Leisha out in a few days to collect it...unless, of course, you have a change of heart about being my ghost."

It was just as Leisha had predicted. Roan felt a thrill of excitement at the thought of her coming to the cottage...alone. He knew it would be the beginning of something that neither one of them would have the power to stop. He wondered if Darien Port understood that he was sealing their fate with his own blessing.

Late into the night, Roan stayed up with Darien Port's manuscript, entering the haunting, powerful dimensions of his mind. Reading the words was like entering some whirling vortex. The story did not quite come together. Even if he had wanted to, Roan knew nothing he could do would ever complete what was an extension of the old man's soul. Darien Port was the only one who could ever make it whole.

Roan thought about his own unformed novel, the budding words just beginning to take shape and grow. He knew what he must do. For once in his life he would keep his promise to himself, make this the summer of his own success. He would return Darien Port's manuscript to him with his apologies.

Roan had the manuscript bundled and waiting on his desk when Leisha appeared at his door one evening. She must have walked to his cabin, though the distance was greater than a mile. As if oblivious to the chill air, she wore only a thin, sheath-like dress of antique white silk. Her skin seemed to match the hue of the fabric, to take on its pearly sheen. The cascade of hair against so much paleness seemed even darker. Her eyes were a deeper shade of green.

"I've decided to return the manuscript," Roan said. He turned to lift it from the nearby table, to offer it to her, but she had slipped past him into the bedroom. He heard the rustle of falling silk.

"Leisha—" All protests died from his lips at the sight of her lying upon his bed, arms reaching out to him invitingly. As he twined his fingers in her long, dark hair, all thoughts of Darien Port and the manuscript scattered.

Weak with desire, he felt the touch of her lips, her hands. He felt her move with him, leading him to ecstasy. Throes of desire muffled his cries as a razor-sharp pain pierced his neck, followed by a hot surge of blood. When she had satisfied his hunger, in the thrall of pleasure and pain, he watched her feed.

When she was sated, her eyes were devoid of all color, black as night, the shade of death.

Roan woke feeling spent and exhausted. His head ached.

The unfamiliar taste of wine was stale in his mouth. He gave a little groan. Then he caught sight of Leisha, fully dressed, gazing tenderly down at him, like an angel of mercy. She had brought him a cool glass of water, and once he drank it, he felt much better.

He caught her pale hand, studying the slender fingers, the half-moons of the long, unpolished nails that had raked his back. "You are my muse, my inspiration. Don't go back to him," he pleaded.

She stroked his damp brow. "I will never leave you."

A vague sense of guilt and honor made Roan insist, "Darien must be told."

Leisha, as if unable to bear to part with him for even a moment, insisted on going with him that evening to face Darien Port. A short time later, they stood together at the threshold to the country house. Darien did not invite them in.

As Roan placed the manuscript firmly into Darien's hands, a tinge of irony crossed the old man's face. "So you are returning my manuscript, but not my lovely Leisha?"

Roan met his gaze bravely. "Leisha wants to be with me."

Roan glanced at the woman by his side, and what he saw momentarily chilled him. The look she gave Darien was triumphant, mocking. Again, he saw the green of her pupils dissolve into flecks of silver.

Darien's gaze moved from Leisha to Roan and he spoke softly, "They say all's fair in love and war."

"No hard feelings, then?"

"She can be a curse as well as a blessing. You'll see."

They left together, Leisha clinging so tightly to Roan's arm he could feel a bruise forming.

Roan felt spent, exhausted. Time seemed to blur until dream and waking were all one endless haze. This morning he had made coffee and tried to write a few pages, but every time he started making progress, she was there, rubbing his neck, stroking his hair. Her ever-intoxicating presence had once again broken his concentration and lured him away from his work. But now she slept, and he could return to his writing.

Except no words would come. His mind was a bleak wasteland, an empty void. Roan covered his forehead with his hands as a terrible throbbing pierced the area behind his eyes. Just when he thought he couldn't feel any more miserable, the phone rang.

It was April.

"I know I promised not to call and disturb your work, but I just had to talk to you!" Her voice sounded high and breathless, like the voice of a child. He listened to her prattle with a feeling of disconnection. She could have been a perfect stranger.

Sensing his lack of response, she asked finally, "Roan? You seem a million miles away. Is something wrong?"

"Nothing," he replied shortly. Nothing he could make April understand.

"Maybe I should drive out."

"No!" He knew his response sounded harsh and gruff. But he couldn't deal with it, the intrusion of the outside world, not today.

"I'll call later, then." April was hurt. But she would believe he was upset because she had disturbed his self-imposed isolation. She would never dream another woman lay at that very moment in his bed. He could hardly believe it himself.

Roan's gaze moved back to Leisha, the woman who had captivated him, who he had stolen, and who now waited only for him. She stretched leisurely, like a contented cat, and smiled. "Was the call important, my Darling?"

"It was no one. No one at all." He pushed the manuscript aside and went to her. Why should he waste the day working? Instead they would drink more wine, make love, celebrate both her emancipation and his own.

The phone rang later that day. Probably April again, but Roan didn't bother to answer. He would deal with her later. Right now, nothing was on his mind but Leisha...Leisha...Leisha.

"What's wrong with you, Roan?" his agent demanded. "You don't answer the phone, don't return our calls. April's been worried sick."

"I've been busy," Roan replied shortly. He added with a touch of cynicism, "I'm writing the Great American Novel. Remember?"

A long pause, then the terse response, "Well, It had better be good." The connection severed with an angry click.

In truth, Roan didn't know whether his manuscript was good or not, because, for the most part, it remained unwritten. Almost the end of summer, and still the writer's block was lodged in his brain like some heavy, immovable stone. Roan spent the precious moments while Leisha slept aimlessly wandering about the lake or at his desk, crumpling and tearing up sheet after sheet of paper, desperate to make a chip in the unresisting substance of the stone.

This morning he had left the house early. He needed to be alone. A deeper chill filled the air as Roan made a circle of the shoreline. Not a ripple disturbed the smooth surface of the lake. The mallards had moved on.

Roan attempted to keep a steady pace. Once he had run the entire path with vigor; now he was aware of an all-encompassing weakness. The exertion left him breathless, trembling, on the verge of collapse. The ache in his lungs was like a knife. But still he pressed on, searching, inviting that burst of inspiration.

In the clouds around him, in the glassy reflection of the lake, a vision formed. He stopped, crying out in horror. Wherever he looked, he saw only her face.

There was no escape from her. From the beginning, he had got it all wrong. Leisha had never been the victim, but the tormentor. Darien had passed this curse on to him, had made Roan his living ghost!

He sank to his knees as Leisha moved gracefully as if she floated on mist toward him. "Leave me alone!" he cried, his voice a blind shriek.

Roan could feel himself spiraling downward, sinking toward the very pit of despair. What happened, he wondered, when you finally reached the bottom? He no longer cared; he welcomed death.

An incessant pounding, like the thundering of horses in his head, roused him from his lethargic stupor. He reacted by covering his ears with his hands, but the noise persisted. Finally, Roan stumbled to the door and opened it a crack. Like a prisoner newly released from some dark cell, he shielded his eyes from the unaccustomed light.

Outside stood Darien Port. Roan could only stand and gape at him. Weary lines had vanished from Darien's face, removing years. He looked refreshed, vigorous, as if a heavy burden had been lifted from his heart. "It is finished!" he boomed in a strong and robust voice.

"What...is finished?"

"The manuscript, of course. My final book, my masterpiece!"

Roan blinked dully. "What do you mean?"

"I'm ready to take her back now," Darien said. With a sense of revulsion the old man studied Roan's thin, wasted face, the uncut hair, the hollows that burned beneath his eyes. The marks on his neck and throat stood out like bruises against his white skin. "And none too soon, by the looks of you."

From the corner of the room, Leisha glared at Darien, and her eyes flashed silver. Her long nails curled into cat's claws and she hissed.

"It's no use," Roan responded bleakly. "You were right. She is no muse, she's a monster."

"You cannot blame her, any more than you could blame a cat for stalking a mouse." Darien spoke with surprising empathy. "She's not human, you know. She comes from a race older than mankind."

"She's a vampire."

"Yes, but one that feeds not only upon the body, but upon the soul."

No matter how absurd his words sounded, Roan knew the old man spoke the truth. "She requires a host. She cannot exist unless she feeds off the blood, the thoughts and dreams, the very essence of others."

"And I have become that host."

Darien's steady gaze met Roan's. "She has no choice...no free will of her own. If I call her, she will come with me."

"You would take her back?" Roan gasped, clutching at a slender thread of hope.

Darien bowed his silvery head. "The truth is, I am lonely. I miss her."

"She will destroy you."

"No. My will is too strong. I have learned to control her, to share my life-giving sustenance so that we both may survive." Darien seemed a man at peace with himself. "My work is complete now. I can give her what she wants, what she needs, my full and undivided attention."

"It's no use!" Roan cried out, "She'll never leave me."

Darien looked beyond him. "Come, my Darling," he said gently, extending a hand. "It's time to go home."

As if pulled by some invisible chain, Leisha moved sulkily forward. If he looked closely, her body seemed to shimmer, to subtly change form. Roan wondered vaguely how Darien saw her, his distraction, his torment, his ideal woman. She followed him meekly now, stealing only one wistful, backward glance at Roan. To him, her eyes were and always would be a deep, emerald green.

Girls Who Lie Down With Wolves
By Vicki Britton

Devyn is a troubled Romeo searching for his Juliet...but Juliet no longer wants to play his game.

When Angie heard that Devyn Gray had been released from prison, she told herself she didn't care because it had nothing to do with her anymore. The past five years he had grown more and more unreal until his features were permanently immersed in shadow. Yet every time the doorbell rang she would find her heart pounding at fever pitch. And the nights were worse. The nights made her restless.

"What's wrong?" Hallon would ask, disturbed by her tossing and turning.

"I hear the baby crying."

"I don't hear anything," Hallon would mumble, tossing one arm over her as he drifted back to sleep.

The arm would be like a dead weight. Angie would lie awake, listening. Or if she slept, she would dream about Devyn and the promise. "Forever," she would hear him say, and his voice was more real to her than his face, which she seemed to see as if through a dark mirror.

"Forever," she could hear her own voice respond. She would wake to find that, in sleep, her right hand had crept to her left wrist, softly rubbing the faint marks of the old scar. And she would wake with a sense of horror, still stroking the scar, remembering.

Some girls dream of knights in white armor, but Angie knew that when her love came, he would be riding a motorcycle, the wind racing through his hair.

As soon as he walked in the door, she could smell trouble. It followed him in through the glass door of her Dad's saddle shop along with the dry Arizona heat. At first, she thought he had come to rob her, which was absurd considering that there was less than fifty dollars in the register. She was alone in the store. Afternoons were slow; no customers had come in since early morning, when the man from Vista Hiking Trails had brought in a broken binding for repair. Something about the stranger's eyes made her wary. They were bright brown with a reddish cast. Wolf's eyes.

It wasn't just the eyes that bothered her. His hair was long, choppy, and the black color didn't match the eyes. But it must have been natural; no way could it have been dyed, not with those thick, dark brows.

"What do you want?" she demanded, making her voice sharp for fear that, if she didn't, it would rise high and betray the beginning edges of fear.

"I want to saddle my hoss." He planted both hands down confidently upon the glass counter, above the display of turquoise rings, cuff links, and bracelets they sold to tourists. She could see the veins in his arms, visible along with the lean, tanned cords of muscle. On one forearm was a tattoo that read "Born to—was it

Born to ride or Born to die?—in spirals of blue and black, the last word covered by a portion of dark sleeve.

"You don't look like no cowboy," she challenged, her eyes following the lines of the brown motorcycle jacket, the boots and tight jeans, the silver chain about his neck. A renegade, maybe. The grinning rebel from some late-night James Dean movie. He wasn't really handsome, but his smile was deadly with the kind of charm that always made a girl's heart skip a beat.

He tossed the too-dark hair back, away from his eyes. "Come out, then, if you don't believe me. Come see my horse."

"You're joking," she said, incredulous.

"No, I'm not."

Curiously, she stepped over to the glass window. Out front was parked the ugliest motorcycle she had ever seen.

"Come ride with me. What's your name?"

"Angie."

"Angie, Angel." He moved in so close that they were almost touching. "I like that."

She blushed a little. He was so obviously coming on to her. Was he like this with every girl he met? "Look, what do you want?"

"I saw what I wanted through that big picture window."

His brown eyes were bold and luminous. She wondered if the shine in them was natural.

"You."

Angie scowled, but a tiny thrill, a shiver, coursed through her just the same.

"I want to take you for a ride." He took her hand. Spirals of warmth, heat, seemed to rise from her palm where his fingers traced a light circle upon her skin.

Angie jerked her hand away, as if she had been burned. "I can't." She was intrigued by this stranger, so bold and outspoken, so different from any of the boys she knew in school. "I'm not supposed to leave the shop 'til five."

He shrugged. "I can wait."

His waiting made her nervous, the way he paced the floor like some flighty beast in a too-small cage. He studied the turquoise rings behind the glass, the rows of saddles and fine leatherwork, the silver spurs that hung upon the wall. Afternoon heat made the scent of leather permeate the air.

Angie stalled, posting the last few sales in the ledger. She glanced up at the clock. "I guess I could close up a little early."

A grin spread across his face. His teeth were slightly uneven, but white, even though he smoked. She could see the outline of a package of cigarettes in his pocket. "That's my girl."

"I'm not your girl," she retorted with a defiant shake of her long hair.

Angie knew instinctively that he would drive fast, so she tightened her arms around his waist. His muscles were lean and firm, and she liked the scent of smoke and leather, the electric sense of excitement that filled the air. She knew that she should never have gotten on the bike with him. He could be anyone; he could take her anywhere. But the heat was lazy, the sky blue overhead, and on such a day she could not make herself believe in danger.

They drove up the steep, cliff-lined road that led out to the lake. A bright yellow sun slid over the water, reflecting their images like sheets of mirror glass as they stood at the water's edge. He put his arm around her. "We look as if we belong together," he said, staring at their joined image in the water.

They were about the same height, their hair nearly the same color, but Angie knew that was not what he meant. They seemed a perfect match. Maybe it was simply because he was everything she was not, and their differences complemented each other, like two halves making a whole.

The ripples made their reflections dance. "We look like ghosts in the water," she laughed.

"The ghosts of lovers. Romeo and Juliet. Bonnie and Clyde. Will you be my lover, conquer the world with me?"

She didn't resist when he drew her close, raised her mouth to his, and kissed her. His lips were warm, claiming, possessive, when they had no right to be. She could feel the leather of his jacket against the cotton of her blouse, his hands sliding along her back, searching for an opening in the material, some means of entrance. She knew that it would happen; it was inevitable, but she could not let it happen so soon.

She pulled away, began to run from him, but took two steps and stumbled upon one of the sharp rocks. She glared up at him. "Now look what you made me do!"

He knelt down beside her. "I'm sorry." He stroked her scratched knee through the rip in her jeans. "I didn't mean to hurt you. I'd never want to hurt you."

Her lower lip trembled. "Why don't you take me home?"

"I will." The odd-colored eyes flickered across hers. "But only if I can see you tonight."

"Are you kidding? I can't go out with you!"

He widened his eyes in mock surprise. "What's wrong with me?"

She could imagine the shock in her mother's eyes when he appeared upon the porch of their neat, ranch-style home, a cigarette dangling from his lips. She could see the rest of the tattoo on his forearm now. It said Born to love. "Mothers don't usually go in for the Hell's Angel's type."

His smile was cat-like, lazily appealing. "I don't want to date your Mama."

"Look, you don't know my mother. Or my Dad. I just can't go."

"So, slip out the window."

Angie hesitated. She had never crept around behind her parents' backs. He made it sound simple, easy, as if no moral question were involved.

"I'm sorry. I can't."

They rode back to town in silence. "You can let me off here," she said, pointing to the 7-11.

"If you change your mind, I'll meet you here. At midnight." His gaze burned fire into hers. "The witching hour."

Unsavory characters hung around the 7-11 at night. Angie felt furtive, interested eyes upon her. She checked her watch. Twelve-twenty-five. Why had she come here? She averted her gaze from the punks who hung around the video machines. She thought about bolting, running home.

The roar of the bike seemed deafening, and then he was there beside her, her gallant knight, her dark prince.

"Hello, Beautiful."

She felt a mixture of triumph and relief. The creeps in the 7-11 slipped back into the woodwork, no longer menacing.

"The night is ours," he said. "So what shall we do with it?"

"I don't know."

"I'll take you around, then." The bold smile flashed. "Show you off to some of my friends."

As they drove down Main Street he waved to people, exchanging some secret form of greeting with one of the bearded Night Rovers who parked their bikes in a solid row near the big mall.

A bearded man flagged him down. He stopped the bike. "Business before pleasure. This'll only take a minute."

Angie felt uncomfortable on the street corner, leaning against the bike, waiting. She wondered fleetingly what her parents would think if they happened to see her there, wearing her clinging top and short black skirt, waiting for this man.

"There. All done."

Devyn next stopped in front of a house with broken porch and chipped, white paint. The inside was even more grim and rundown than the outside. "Dad works nights," he explained, "and drinks days. So I've got the run of the place."

A brown-haired girl, who looked barely more than fourteen, came up to greet them. She wore several necklaces and her fingers were studded with rings.

"This is Lissa," Devyn introduced. "She's been staying with us."

"Are you Dev's new girl?" she asked with a flutter of blue-shadowed lids.

Lissa brought out some beer and potato chips. The three others in the room paid them no attention. "That's Barry," Devyn said over the blare of some heavy metal band. Devyn moved toward the boy who lay sprawled out asleep on the couch and gave him a sharp tap with his boot.

"Damn!" The boy named Barry woke cursing, his eyes red and bloodshot beneath a tangle of wiry blond hair. "What do you want, Dev?"

"Got something for you." He tossed a plastic pouch down upon the boy's chest.

The angry words dissipated into a mindless grin.

"Those two fools are Randy and Jo."

Angie nodded, her eyes carefully avoiding the half-clothed couple huddled in a heated embrace beneath the big sleeping bag in the corner.

Devyn shrugged. "What can I say? They're in love."

Angie glanced around at the chaos of beer and Coke bottles, the stubbed ashes of cigarettes. A house without rules. She thought of her own cozy little home with Mom's designer curtains hanging at the windows.

Devyn seemed suddenly restless, embarrassed for both of them. "Let's get out of here. There's a place I want to show you."

The bike roared up the steep, now-familiar trail that led to the lake. Dev took her to a small cave. Within was a small nest of sleeping bag, pillows and blankets. "Sometimes I stay out here," he told her. "It's the only place I can feel like myself, the only place I feel free."

"It suits you. It's sort of like a wolf's lair."

"I am a wolf." He threw back his head and howled into the air. "C'mon, howl with me."

"You're crazy!" She wanted to laugh, but instead she joined him. Their voices blended in the night air, echoed back to them across the lake.

He pulled her into his arms, and together they sank down upon the pile of blankets. She thought of the couple in the house, making love, oblivious to the presence of a total stranger.

"I'm not like you and your friends. I mean, I'm not sure this is going to work out."

"You like me, don't you? You like being with me. And I like you."

"It's not that simple."

"Sure it is." He covered her face with kisses. "I want you, Angie."

She stopped the hands that reached for her in the darkness. "You and me, we're from different worlds, Dev."

It's OK," he whispered. He slipped the heavy silver chain from his neck. On the end of it was the metal likeness of some fierce animal. Was it a wolf? "This is my symbol. This is me." Ceremoniously, he looped the chain around her neck. "This means we belong together. After tonight, you'll be mine."

Angie thought of Lissa's adoring eyes. Many girls she knew would die to be in her place. To them, maybe even to her, Devyn Gray represented excitement, danger, a certain kind of power.

"Forever?"

"Wolves mate forever," he replied, his eyes deep and golden. "And they always protect their own."

When his lips sought hers, Angie pushed her doubts and fears into the corner of her mind. She lost touch with time and reality, which seemed to mean nothing at all now that she was in his arms.

He caught her close to him, holding the sides of her face, his hands caressing her long hair. "I've always been alone, you know. Mom running off, Dad always drinking."

"Oh, Devyn—" Angie kissed his bare chest in the moonlight. With his long hair tumbling over his face and shoulders, the wide, dark eyes, he looked like some orphaned boy.

He tugged at the silver chain shining around her neck. "You won't ever leave me, will you?"

"Never," she promised.

Angie twisted the silver chain about her neck, and felt a little shiver. Whoever he was, whatever he was, she had cast her lot with Devyn Gray. It was too late for caution now.

The next few days, Devyn hung around the saddle shop, sitting with her behind the counter. When the store was empty, they kissed and held hands and once, in the tiny back storeroom, they made love.

Angie was straightening her hair and skirt when her father unexpectedly appeared. His sharp eyes moved from Angie, then to Devyn, then back to his daughter again. She flushed, embarrassed, afraid that he could somehow read guilt in her eyes.

"I came by for the deposit," he said.

The weekly bank deposit, which her father always figured on Thursday nights, was in a white envelope beneath the cash register drawer.

"This is Devyn," Angie said finally. "A friend of mine."

Her dad nodded curtly. Without a word, back stiff, he left the store.

"I think he likes me," Dev commented wryly.

"Like I said before, you're every father's dream."

"Every father's dream, every mother's nightmare." He winked at her. "Let's go back into the storeroom."

"No, Dev. What if someone comes in?"

Angie had reason to be grateful for her caution. A short time later, her father unexpectedly returned.

"There's fifty dollars missing from this deposit," he announced grimly.

"Are you sure?"

"The teller counted it twice."

"Maybe you made a mistake in addition last night."

"I never make mistakes." His voice turned cold.

"Dad, surely you don't think I took the money."

"Not you. Him." His gray eyes were so dark they seemed almost black as he pointed at Devyn. "I want you out of my store, Punk. Now!"

"Look, I didn't take your money."

Her father took a menacing step toward him. "Get out!"

"I don't have your money!" He met him impudently, with outstretched arms. "Go ahead and search me!"

For a moment, the two of them glared at each other; they seemed to be snarling at each other like two lions about to join in battle.

Muscles bulged in her father's neck and throat; she could see the pulse pound at his temple. She glanced at Devyn, suddenly afraid of him, of the defiant half-smile and glittering eyes. Frozen behind the counter, feeling caught between them, she watched Devyn's hands curl up into fists. "Dev, no!"

"Get out before I call the police," her father warned.

With a last look at Angie, Dev sullenly left the shop.

Angie's dad brought his fist down upon the counter top. "That boy is bad news. I don't ever want to see him in here again. I don't want you having anything to do with him!"

"But Dad—"

He turned his back on her.

Angie had expected as much. How could he possibly understand? Despite her parents' love and the cozy little house, at times Angie felt just as alone as Devyn Gray.

That night, Angie slipped out to meet Dev as usual, but some of the excitement had worn thin.

"You don't believe that stuff your dad told you?" Devyn asked. As he spoke, he toyed with the pocketknife he always carried. His eyes shone like fierce red stars in the moonlight. "You don't think I took the money?"

Angie didn't answer.

"Someone could have come in while we were in the back room."

"I didn't hear anyone, did you?"

A strange look crossed Devyn's face. "Maybe your old man took the money out himself. Did you ever think of that?"

"Why would he do that?"

"To make you doubt me."

Angie considered. It was just the kind of trick her father would pull. Yet she could not bring herself to be angry. She knew her dad only wanted to protect her.

"So did it work? Do you doubt me?"

"No."

He grinned. "Good. I'm glad you're not going to let him come between us. I don't want anyone to ever come between us."

The grin disappeared. "Sometimes I feel like the whole world's turned against me, Angie." He reached out to touch her hair. "And then there's you." His eyes met hers, soft and warm. "You're the only one I can trust, the only one I can depend on." A darkness fell over his face. "I keep having this feeling that something bad is going to happen to me."

"Don't talk like that, Dev. It frightens me."

"I could almost kill myself." Calmly, he pressed the blade of the knife into his wrist, drawing a thin line of blood.

"Dev, no!" Fear spread across Angie's face.

She watched the knife move across his skin, her initials appear in blood. "I'd die if it wasn't for you."

She held her arm out to him. "Mark me, too."

"Are you sure?"

She felt the sharp sting of the blade as it slashed quickly, skillfully across her wrist. The pain felt numb and deep, like the scrape of a razorblade. He raised her wrist to his and pressed them together until their blood mingled. "Nothing can separate us now. We're bound by blood."

"I love you," Dev," she whispered.

Yet when they made love, she had the strange sensation that she had crawled out of her body and was watching someone else, arms and legs entwined about some frightening stranger. The time she spent with Dev belonged to another dimension, surreal, a fantasy land. She lived in multiple worlds, worlds in layers, and he was only a part of one of them.

Monday morning, Angie stared in horror at the shattered door and windows. The saddle shop had been broken into during the weekend. The glass counter was wrecked, the turquoise and money from the cash register gone.

The first thought that entered her head was that Dad would blame Dev.

She had to find Dev, to warn him. The curves of the road were slippery and a time or two the wheels of her father's Chevy slipped on loose gravel as she veered too close to the edge of the steep embankment.

The cave was deserted, but he would be back. The sleeping bag and blankets were still there. Angie shivered a little, hugging her arms to her chest as she stepped from the shelter of gray rock. Without Dev, the lake was a desolate, lonesome place.

Angie drove back to town, searching for the house Dev had taken her to the night she'd first gone with him. She recognized the chipped white paint, the broken steps of the sagging porch.

Lissa's face peered out at her, the eyes curious and round beneath thick mascara.

"Is Devyn here? I need to talk to him—"Angie's voice trailed off as she stared at Lissa's hand, which now rested on the doorframe. A wave of shock ran through her. On Lissa's finger was a bright blue turquoise ring, one she recognized from the glass case at the shop.

Angie visited Devyn once in jail before they transferred him to the state facility. The police had picked him up on possession of narcotics and several counts of robbery.

"They're sending me to prison," he said, the red-gold eyes mocking, as if they still ruled the world. "Can you believe it?"

She did not reply. She only looked at him, noticing how the shadows of the bars distorted his features. She had loved him because he was free, and now he was as confined as a person could possibly be. How did wolves live in captivity? Did they pace the floor and eventually die?

Angie finally spoke. "I can see how you could cheat a drug dealer or even a stranger, but how could you lie to me, how could you steal from me?

"I never lied to you, Angie. I didn't take the money."

"You broke into the store."

"I was mad at your father for accusing me. I wanted to get even."

"By destroying my father's business? Didn't you even think about me? Don't you care that what you did really hurt me?"

"Will you wait for me, Angie?"

Hadn't he heard a word of what she had said? "I'm the one who turned you in, you bastard. I'm the one who sent them to the cave to find you." Angie jerked at the chain around her neck, but the pendant, the silver wolf's head, wouldn't come off. With fingers that trembled with hurt and rage she finally managed to unhook the clasp and toss the pendant at him.

"Do you really think it's that easy? We've started something that can't be stopped."

"I hate you!" she cried.

"I can't help being who I am, what I am." His face looked gaunt and shadowed through the bars. "I love you, Angie. I'll love you forever."

She whirled and ran away. Behind her, Angie could hear him shaking the bars, and his cries were not unlike the anguished howls of a wolf.

When Devyn Gray came for her, Angie felt the numb disbelief of one who has complacently ignored storm warnings to find herself thrust suddenly into the heart of a violent tornado.

It was a hot, drowsy afternoon, the kind of day when even the weather denies any threat of danger. Hal was out of town on a business trip. The baby was at her mother-in-law's across town. Angie was enjoying a peaceful afternoon when the buzzer rang. With no thought of caution, she stepped over to the door and opened it wide.

He was standing outside. For a moment, she was speechless.

She stood listening to the thunder in her ears, the sound of her familiar world shattering and falling apart all around her.

Devyn. Five years had made slight difference. The dark hair was shorter, the skin a little paler. Prison-pale. He wasn't handsome, but then had he ever been handsome, even when she had loved him?

"Angel." The way he said her name made her ache. He stared at her, and the places his eyes touched felt scorched, as if he still had the power to burn them.

"What—what are you doing here?" Angie forced herself to face him, this familiar stranger. She would not let see him that she was afraid. She would get to the phone, call the police, call someone. But who did you call when your past rises up to threaten the future?

"I want you to come with me, Angie."

His words made her shiver. He was her black knight, their romance a dream where at the end the hero either dies or changes. But he had done neither. And he was here to claim her.

She tried to close the door on him, but he pushed it back with a strength that frightened her. He entered the house where he stood, a dark intruder on the threshold of bright, cozy rooms.

She held her breath as his gaze settled upon a framed picture of Hallon. "Is he the reason?"

He took up the picture and smashed it against the edge of the coffee table. Visions of the ruined saddle shop, of shattered wood and broken glass struck fear into Angie's soul. His rage seemed to fill the empty space all around them.

Angie shielded her eyes with her hands to avoid looking at the smiling, shattered face of Hallon upon the floor between them. "Please, just go away!"

As he advanced toward her, his hand slipped into his jacket pocket, drew out a dark object. A gun. "I don't want to hurt you, Angie," he said with measured calmness. "I only want you to come with me."

Time stopped. Fear squeezed the breath from her lungs. "Please, Devyn," she pleaded. "I've built a life here. Won't you just go away and forget about me?"

Something terrible flickered in those hot, golden eyes; a haunted, helpless look. "I can't."

He stepped back and held the door as they went outside.

The motorcycle waited in bright sunlight. Like one in a trance, she got on behind him. The feel of the wind, the rough leather of his jacket, was both familiar and frightening. Devyn drove faster and faster until the wind lashed her hair across her face, stinging like a thousand tiny whips. She recognized the rough, winding road, sheltered on one side by a high, smooth wall of rock. He was taking her to the cave.

Angie thought weakly of the gun which was now tucked into his pocket. Did he plan to kill her, maybe even kill them both? The love they had once shared had become a living thing, twisted, evil, a monster of his own creation.

Devyn lived in a fantasy world, a world of madness, and he was forcing her against her will to join him. A rush of hatred made the adrenaline pump through Angie's blood, momentarily blotting out the fear. She no longer belonged to his past, but to her own future. She was not going to let him destroy her!

Angie watched the road, waiting for a sharp twist which would force Devyn to slow the bike. She felt his muscles tense as he leaned into a deep curve. Bracing herself for a fall, Angie purposefully made her body go limp as she attempted to slide from the bike.

The bike wobbled as Devyn fought for control. She heard the spray of pebbles, the grating squeal of the tires as they came dangerously close to the edge of the embankment. She was forced to cling tightly to him as he righted the bike and drove on with reckless speed. She could only close her eyes and hold on to him, helpless and afraid.

The way grew steeper, the bike beneath them trembled, as

they climbed the steep rise. Angie waited for another chance.

The motorcycle, jolting against rocks, continued to lose momentum. Midway up the incline, Angie tore her hands away from Devyn's waist. She propelled herself backward, struggling to maintain her balance and land on her feet. Instead she struck hard against the gravel, pain racking through her body.

Still, she had managed to break free.

Stunned, she watched Devyn slow the bike. He turned around once and looked at her, as if through a void of space and time. Then the deafening roar of the bike's engine pierced the air.

In silent horror she watched the bike slam over the steep stone embankment. Breathless, Angie made her way to the edge of the cliff already knowing what she would see: the wrecked bike with it spinning tires, Devyn's still form sprawled out upon the rocks beside it.

Limping, Angie climbed down the rocks until she reached him.

She would call the wreck an accident, an act of madness. But in the end, she knew that he had made the sacrifice, had severed the only way he knew how the terrible bond between them. He had set her free.

The pendant of the wolf's head that Devyn always wore glinted in the sunlight. As her fingers closed around it his words came back to her, "Wolves mate forever. And they always protect their own."

Kinfolk
By Vicki Britton

A party at the old ghost town sounds like fun for a group of teenagers...until the ghosts appear.

There will be another party at our house tonight. We can see the group of teenagers now, from the upstairs window. The same bunch as before, five or six of them crammed into one blue sports car.

Clem curses as we watch the intruders twist, bump, and wind their way down the deeply rutted dirt road, then pull to a stop in front of the old churchyard. In a matter of minutes they have all struggled out of the car and are headed toward our house by way of the church.

"The nuisances." Clem mutters as one of them hurries with eager steps into the sacred place, long empty of any congregation save the night birds, the field mice and us.

"Brothers," cries the bold one.

"Blasphemy!" Clem mutters, turning away as the youngster begins to preach a mock sermon.

"We are gathered here today to praise the Lord!" His voice echoes hollowly through the evening darkness.

"Hallelujah!" chorus the two other boys. They follow close behind the first, lugging that inevitable case of beer.

"Come on, it's too cold to play games," says one of the two girls. "Let's build a campfire before we all freeze."

"Let's get the sleeping bags and stay in the church tonight."

"No." The blond girl's voice rang high and frightened. "This is a church. Or, at least, it was. And that old cemetery out back gives me the creeps."

"Let's go to that rickety house, then," says the boy she is with. "The one with the neat chimney."

"But..." The dark-haired boy who has been quiet up to now begins to speak. "That's where..."

"Shh..." the bold one cuts him off. He walks over to the quiet one and I hear him whisper, "The girls don't know what happened there. They'd be afraid if they did and they'd want to go home."

And so, they come to our house, bringing with them an endless trail of potato chips and beer.

"Kids these day!" Clem gripes as they begin to come in through the broken door, disregarding the boarded windows, the NO TRESPASSING, THIS MEANS YOU sign hanging at an awkward angle upon the sagging, barbed wire fence.

Clem has never been known for his patience. He watches restlessly now, thin arms folded across his chest, as the little group begins to lay out their sleeping bags upon the dusty, barren floor. One steps over to our huge stone fireplace and begins to stack the wood someone left from the last camp-out.

"Now they'll be up till all hours of the night, laughin' and drinkin' and tellin' them bawdy tales," Clem grumbles. I shiver at the strange light that has come into his eyes. "Unless we stop them. Tonight. I say it ought to be tonight!"

I don't say anything, but I see that Clem's eyes have strayed to the place where the axe is hidden.

The quiet boy has taken his guitar from the case and is strumming lightly. The girl beside him is singing, clapping her hands to the music. I look down and for the first time really notice her. She is dressed in blue jeans, a faded shirt, and an old Army jacket two sizes too big for her. Her hair is long, straight, and the soft kind of brown that shines golden in the glow of the crackling firelight. Her eyes are brown, too. Big, dark, and gentle like Sara's.

Clem and I never speak of Sara anymore. We haven't, not since that terrible day when the Indians took her away with them. Clem and I, we couldn't leave here and find her. We're just poor souls stuck in this abandoned town, stuck like flies in a bottle.

But the loneliness lingers. That's why I don't mind the young folks as much as Clem does. Because of Sara, I guess.

The music and laughter mingle with the natural sounds of the night; the creaking of rotted floorboards, the rush of the wind through the spindly branches of trees along empty streets. The natural sounds increase in volume as the singing stops and their voices become hushed.

The bold one is telling a gruesome tale about the hobo who was seen floating facedown in the creek one hot day last summer. "A couple of young hikers discovered him. Dead as a log, he was. When the police came, they found his sleeping bag and a wallet with twenty dollars in it, right here in this very house. But when they went back to the creek, the body was gone. It vanished into thin air!" The boy pauses, then adds with a twinkle in his eyes, "And that's not the only disappearance in this old ghost town. The year before a young girl, a hitchhiker, turned up missing. They found her backpack hanging by the fireplace right over there, but they never found her."

The bold one has finished his tale, and the pretty, brown-haired girl stands up and walks over to the broken window. I see Clem watching her. She is peering out at the few crumbling, abandoned buildings bathed in yellow moonlight. Far off in the distance, a small handful of gravestones glow white in the semidarkness. I am afraid of the thoughts forming in Clem's mind.

"I'm not scared," the girl says, but she sounds scared. "I remember my mother telling me once that some of our kinfolk lived here in this very town. Killed by Indians, so the story goes. My great-great grandmother was the only survivor." She pauses a moment, deep in thought. Then she asks slowly, as if trying to recall a feeling half-forgotten. "Do you think they were happy?"

The one with the guitar takes another slug of beer. "Who?"

"The people who lived and died here."

"What does it matter?" The boy shrugs in a matter-of-fact way, and I can see the muscles in Clem's jaw tighten. "They're all gone now."

The pretty girl frowns, says reflectively, "Their lives, our lives. How long is eternity?"

"We've only got now, Beth. So stop worrying yourself with questions. And stop shivering. Come back over here by the fire."

Their voices fall silent, leaving only the rushing sound of the wind and the crackling of dying embers. They have all gone to sleep, half-drunk and happy, curled up in their sleeping bags like caterpillars in their cocoons.

Then Clem is standing over her, the sleeping girl, and she stirs lightly as if disturbed by a dream. I pray silently, holding my breath. Not her, not this sweet, brown-haired girl! Surely, he hasn't chosen her! Clem, remember our Sara!

Then I begin to think an evil thought. Wouldn't it be nice to have her here with us forever? It would be nice to have a girl around, blood relation. We could even call her Sara instead of Beth.

Clem stands for a long time, just watching her sleep. Then he turns away. "We can't. She's kinfolk. Come, Millie," he whispers, and there is an age-old sadness in his eyes. "Let's go to bed."

Dawn arrives and they are leaving. Only streaks of light cross the horizon. Through the dimness I can see that they are all out by the car except for Beth. She, alone, finishes rolling up her sleeping bag, packing her blanket and jacket with lingering hands. Finally, she, too, stands, pausing a moment at the window. "I wish I could have known my ancestors who once lived here," she says, her voice sounding small and sincere.

"Goodbye, Child, goodbye," I whisper, tears burning my eyes.

The brown-haired girl turns suddenly, dark eyes wide. She cocks her head as if listening, although I know she cannot hear me.

"What's the matter, Beth?" calls the young man standing outside. "We're waiting for you."

"I thought...I thought for a moment I heard something. But it must have been the breeze blowing in through the crevices."

He takes her hand and helps her crawl over the barbed wire fence.

"You know, there really is something strange about this old house," I hear her say as they walk through the silent streets to the waiting car, to another waiting century.

"Pretty spooky, huh?" the boy says with a crooked grin. "We'll have to party out here again sometime."

"No, not me. I don't think I'll ever come back."

I can feel Clem's presence beside me, soft and light like a whisper of wind through the cemetery. I follow him past the rows of graves with their bone-white markers. On some the earth is cracked and dry; on others it is strangely damp and fresh.

This place is ours. We must keep the outsiders away. That means we must take victims from time to time, but we are always careful whom we choose. The missing hitchhiker has settled into the old house across the street, happier now than she ever was in life. She waves to us as we head back to our own place. Down the street, we meet the old hobo, stumbling his way to the saloon, content in any time, any circumstances, as long as he's got his gin.

As for Clem and I, we are alone again. Alone with the solitary birds and the field mice and the others of our kind. And my heart aches for Sara.

Run If You Can
By Loretta Jackson

The moment Selene asks for a divorce she is stalked by a gunman...one she believes her own husband hired to kill her.

The man had been watching the house ever since Selene had asked Wayne for a divorce. She stepped closer to the picture window in full view of him and met his bleak stare with what she could muster of courage. His tall form, clad in faded jeans and T-shirt lettered Panthers, hunched forward slightly in some grim acknowledgement—no other motion, no pretense of being about any ordinary business.

He stood between the tall oak and the steps, so close she could note the details of his face: the sparse but scruffy beard, the cutting crease between his eyes that gave him a sense of terrible purpose.

The image of the watcher, no doubt someone Wayne had met in one of his frequent trips to the Sixth Street bars, remained locked in her mind as she retreated from the window into the careful arrangement of green vines and plush white couches. Last night she had made the fact clear to Wayne that if he didn't leave, she would. Tammy Dunn: Wayne always went out with the married ones, signaled the final ending of their miserable marriage. Usually Wayne was discreet concerning his lovers, but this one he had flaunted. Tammy was petite and freckled, red-headed; he preferred her—not enough to abandon the great old house Selene inherited from her mother, not enough to quit the corporation, or relinquish the place in the Rimrock community Mother had so reluctantly bestowed upon him.

Wayne had great confidence in his charm, in his ability to hold Tammy and Selene, too. Probably that explained the man outside, some degenerate Wayne was paying to watch her so he could easily find her if she left.

The next time Selene checked, the watcher had either moved away, blending with the evening shadows, or he was gone. As she looked for him, Wayne, always in a rush, spun the car carelessly into the driveway. His black hair, forever tossed, as if he had been swimming or playing tennis, made him look like some high school quarterback. The sight of his solid body, his perfect features, no longer enchanted her. Instead, Selene steeled herself against his cunning, against his lies.

"Hi, Sel," he said, almost humbly, as if her waiting for him was more than he had expected.

"Your clothes are packed," she said slowly, controlling her anger with great effort.

A smile remained in his eyes to mock her.

"It's up to you to leave. The house is mine."

"What ever happened to ours?" he asked, as if her definite statement had been made merely to amuse him. His first stop was always at the bar, lifting, examining bottles. He mixed a drink.

"I don't want you here, not even for one more night."

Wayne took a step toward her, fingers tight on the glass. "What ever happened to a second chance?"

Selene shrank from the hand that reached out for her. Compliantly, he dropped his arm, attempting to hold her only with his eyes, trying to drown her, as he once had so easily done, in their soulful depths.

"Are you going to leave?"

He shrugged.

"At least be man enough to answer yes or no."

"All right, no."

The matter-of-fact way he spoke infuriated her. "I'll hire someone to move your things to the cabin."

"Then I'll hire someone to move them back. I am not going to leave this house, Sel. You might as well get that straight." Wayne took a sip from his glass before adding, "I'll stay in my half of the house, if that's what you wish." He stared at her a long time before he raised the glass again. "If you're sure that's your wish."

What insufferable egotism. How could it even cross his mind that she would still want him? She controlled a desire to strike out at him, to beat the smile off his face with her fists or with one of the bottles he had placed on the bar.

I hate him. She had never allowed herself to think those words before, but now they screamed into consciousness as if breaking free. In reaction to their force, she backed away from him and hurried up the stairs to the room where she was now sleeping-her mother's old room.

Selene entered feeling defeated. She avoided looking toward her mother's portrait, but it appeared to her nonetheless: the erect head topped with dark curls, the blue eyes reflecting the steel that had kept together the Whitlock Corporation. Mother would not have fled from Wayne or from any opponent. Were they alike only in physical appearance?

Selene sank down in the rocker and wanted to sob. If only she could undo all the mistakes. If she could once again be engaged to Charlie Spann, if she had not caused dissension between her dear mother and herself, had not brought havoc and unrest into the corporation that not even Charlie Spann with his immense skills could stabilize. All in the name of Wayne! Of love! Selene's loathing for Wayne now seemed the result of some cruel justice.

She remained immobile, until time, measured by the slow ticking of the clock on the nightstand, lost all meaning. At last, confused and weary, Selene wandered to the window and looked out into the darkness. Her eyes sought the exact spot where the watcher had stood this afternoon. The thought of him caused her to shiver. He had looked more like a psycho than someone hired for some rational purpose. Only a madman would be so unconcerned about being detected. Was he still out there?

The grounds, a mass of shadows, remained vacant and still. Distant yard lights from neighboring houses made Selene realize the extent of her isolation, jarred her into recalling the fact that for the first time in years she had failed to lock the front door. Wayne would never think of it, even if it were his intent to do so. He left all responsibility up to her.

Just as Selene reached her door, she heard a noise from downstairs, a faint, muffled sound she could not identify. Was it a scrape, a slight rattling? Could it be Wayne? Her heart began to pound. Wayne would not risk harming her himself, but what if he had hired someone to do it for him, someone posing as a robber? Selene would then be out of the way, all of her vast holdings would be his, with the added bonus of Tammy Dunn.

She was being foolish. Wayne, for all his faults, would not kill anyone. Without turning on the hall light, Selene moved down the hallway toward Wayne's room. The door was open. She could make out his form entangled in covers. She listened for his regular, deep intakes of breath. Satisfied that he was asleep, she headed toward the wide stairway and pressed the switch on the nearby wall.

Harsh light flooded the downstairs. She scanned the room for an intruder, for something out of place. Nothing. She was allowing fear to govern her, to call forth noises. She drew a deep breath, steadied herself by gripping the banister, then with quick, direct steps she walked to the front door and snapped the bolt.

Once back in her room, Selene heard another sound. This time it was identifiable, a shifting of weight causing a slight creak on the stairway. This footstep couldn't be Wayne's who she had just seen sleeping in his room. Someone—the man she had seen outside—had definitely entered the house. With every second he was drawing nearer. Selene, with shaking fingers, latched the bolt on her door and in panic sprang toward the phone.

The sheriff had taken their safety seriously; he himself appeared at the door. He looked as if he had just awakened. His crumpled uniform, unbuttoned at the throat, spoke of urgency, of haste.

Bert Abbott's appearing in person paid tribute to a long relationship of Whitlock support, support she never allowed to stop after Mother's death, in spite of the fact that Wayne disliked anyone who was not both well-to-do and white.

Abbott directed his deputy to check the grounds. He listened carefully as Selene told him all she knew about the man who had been keeping such bold surveillance. "I know beyond a doubt," she said, "that he was inside the house when I called you."

The sheriff, immediately accepting her word, began checking the downstairs area.

Wayne, bathrobe wrapped around him, black hair ruffled, appeared at the top of the stairs, calling, "What's going on?"

The sheriff looked for a long time at Selene before telling him. Wayne came down the steps, looping the belt around his slender waist. "Sel, why didn't you awaken me? I don't understand."

The sheriff's questioning look, moving from Wayne to her, darkened with puzzlement.

Something was different about Wayne's manner. His usual rush had vanished leaving an unnatural slowness of voice and movement. Ordinarily he would not follow the sheriff around the house. Wayne always gave orders, but never assistance.

Selene's heart sank. Wayne was playing a role. She had done the very thing he had wanted her to do. Now when the fake robbery did occur, it would all be neatly on record.

What was she believing? That Wayne was actually setting the stage for her murder?

"What did you do after you made the phone call?" the sheriff asked her after he had searched the rooms upstairs.

"I stayed in my room until I saw your vehicle."

"If the intended robber were inside the house, he must have left the way he entered, through the front door. Everything else is locked. I'm going to check with Joe."

Abbott's leaving made Wayne's presence impossible to ignore. She watched him mix a drink. He turned and sounding genuinely concerned, said, "Damned thieves. They're sure getting bold."

Abbott reentered. "Nothing out there." He stood near the door, reluctant to leave. When he finally spoke, he addressed his words to Selene instead of Wayne. "Mrs. Dorrie, it looks to me as if someone's casing the place." His deep voice continued in a slow drawl that increased her terror. "You know Dale Kogler? He was robbed last Monday while he was attending a convention in Piedmont." The sheriff's black eyes narrowed. "It doesn't seem quite the same, somehow. Anyway, we'll patrol, but you must do everything you can to protect yourself."

* * *

As soon as Wayne left for work, Selene called Charlie Spann. Thank God for Charlie! He was always there, like a security with her name on it.

From the first day of their marriage, Wayne had done everything he could do to undermine Charlie's influence with Whitlock Corporation. Wayne's attacks were daily becoming more vicious, but Charlie, a strong opponent, still retained his seat as board chairman and from it firmly directed company policy.

"You sounded frightened," Charlie said as Selene opened the door. He gazed at her, his lean hand reached for hers, warm fingers tightened protectively.

Selene wanted to move into his arms. She would feel safe— she always had—pulled close to his tall, lank body. Instead she stepped away, her hand slipping from his grasp.

Charlie stood near the window in a glare of brightness. Sunlight added a silvery brilliance to his blond hair, intermingled with the light that always appeared in varying degrees in his gray eyes.

"I have to talk to someone. Who else but you."

He sank into a nearby chair. "If you're worried about Dallas, don't be. I fully realize what's at stake." As always his take-charge manner soothed her. "It's going to take more than Dorrie's opposition to keep me away from that meeting."

"It's not Dallas. It's Wayne."

In the quietness Charlie's hand moved upward, stroking his chin, coming to rest at his jawline in a pose of thoughtful patience he so often assumed when listening at board meetings. As Selene told him everything, including her suspicions concerning the watcher, his eyes grew dark and opaque.

Charlie rose and stepped close to her. She could see the crinkles around his gray eyes and remembered the time they had been the quick evidence of a smile. Her whirlwind romance with

Wayne that had ended in a foolish, impulsive marriage had hurt Charlie so very much.

"I love you, Selene." He wiped the tears that had begun to trail down her face, then his lips met hers almost reverently. "Don't worry, I'm going to get us out of this!" He didn't hesitate. "My flight to Dallas leaves at eight o'clock tonight. You're coming with me."

As much as she wanted to, she knew that she couldn't just leave with him.

"Dorrie's capable of anything," Charlie said. "Even murder! The only way to know you're safe is to keep you right with me!"

"I don't want to supply Wayne with any grounds for legal action. I'm afraid if we left together even for a meeting, Wayne would make quite a scandal of it."

"Let him. I want you on that plane tonight."

"There's nothing for you to worry about. I'm not staying in this house any longer. I will check into the Rimrock Hotel. I intend to start divorce proceedings right away."

A fire lit in Charlie's eyes. "Don't think I'm going to stand back and let you handle this all alone. I made one mistake not fighting your decision to marry him! I'm not making another. This time, I'm going to stop Wayne Dorrie dead in his tracks."

Rimrock Hotel, Rimrock's finest, was at best drab and uncomfortable. Selene hated the heavy, gray drapes stagnant with smoke, the view beyond them of weather-stained limestone buildings, their flat-roofs thick with tar.

Thinking she would never file for divorce if he were around to talk her out of it, Wayne would be determined to know her exact whereabouts. No doubt the purpose of the watcher had been to spy on her, not to kill her. The desk clerk had watched curiously as she had signed the register. Where she was staying would not be a secret for very long.

Selene stared down into the street where traffic moved slowly. Her gaze followed the people who walked along the sidewalk. Occasionally she would start, thinking she recognized in some passing form the image of the man who had been stalking her. She grew more and more uneasy, as if she were certain he was out there, as if intense, crazy eyes watched her from some place of concealment.

She checked her watch, five minutes after eight. Charlie would be on his flight to Dallas. How she loved him! If only she were free; if only she could be seated beside him now. She glanced from the window a final time, noting how quickly light was fading from the sky. Feeling more afraid of the gathering darkness outside than of the lonely room, she pulled the drapes closed.

As she did, the phone beside the bed rang shrilly. It hadn't taken Wayne long to locate her. Why didn't he just give her a divorce, take what he could of the money and leave? Was it the prestige, the company position, he didn't want to give up? Selene lifted the receiver, expecting to hear Wayne.

"Mrs. Dorrie, I'm downstairs. I must speak to you." Selene recognized the sheriff's voice before he added, "Sheriff Abbott."

"I'm in room 609. Come on up."

He must have captured the watcher. Thank God! Maybe now she could get a night's sleep. Weariness increased as Selene waited for Abbott in the vacant hallway. She attempted to read the sheriff's expression as he approached. A grimness dulled his eyes, caused him to hesitate.

Her heart pounded.

Abbott passed by her into the room before he spoke. "I hate to be the one to have to tell you this."

"What? What's happened?" Her own voice sounded distant and muffled to her in the silence that followed.

"It's your husband, Mrs. Dorrie."

Selene felt the strength drain from her legs.

"He's dead."

Abbott caught her shoulders and assisted her to the chair. Selene tried to speak, to ask him how Wayne had died. No words came. Abbott continued talking. She could hear his voice, but what he said made no sense to her.

She managed at last to speak. "Was it an accident?"

"I just told you, Mrs. Dorrie. He was shot three times with a .22 revolver." He leaned over her chair. "I'm going to have to ask you some questions." He spoke in a kindly way, but his voice was very firm. "What are you doing here?"

"My husband and I were...planning to divorce." She had been trying not to cry, but tears flowed of their own will down her face. She wiped at them. So the watcher was a robber after all. Wayne must have tried to stop him. She had trouble speaking. "Did you catch the robber, the killer?"

The sheriff straightened up, the look of sympathy replaced by other thoughts. "It's just the way I told you before."

"You'll have to explain it again."

"Your neighbor, Mrs. Corry, reported hearing gun shots. Your front door was open. I went inside and Mr. Dorrie was..." his voice trailed off, then picked up with greater volume, "lying on the floor in the front room. Whoever shot him had escaped out the back door. I couldn't find anything missing or out of place. But it will be necessary for you to return to the house and make a full report."

"I'll go with you now."

"No, not tonight. In fact, don't leave here. I want to know exactly where you are every minute."

Wayne...dead! Selene's mind, totally unable to absorb this turn of events, reeled.

"Your neighbor said she saw you leave home with your

suitcases. I had little trouble locating you. Did you leave the hotel after you checked in?"

Silence this time appeared to be filled with indictment. "No," Selene said.

"Mrs. Corry also told me that right before you left, Charlie Spann stopped by. I traced his whereabouts to the airport, where he bought two tickets. But he didn't get on the plane."

Selene ventured a glance at the sheriff's broad, muscular face. His eyes, a glowing black, the exact color of his skin, had narrowed.

Abbott continued to stare at her. "I wonder who he bought the second ticket for?"

"Why don't you ask him?"

"I will, when and if I find him."

"What is that supposed to mean? Charlie is Whitlock's board chairman. He's not some shoddy transient." It was bad enough to be suspected herself, but she had endangered the one person in the world who meant the most to her. She should have kept Charlie out of this. She tried again to counter Abbott's accusation with what she believed to be the truth. "Wayne was killed by the man who was watching the house."

"After your call last night," the sheriff answered, "I personally combed the whole area. I saw nothing of this man. No one but you, Mrs. Dorrie, has even seen him."

"You surely aren't saying that I made the whole thing up?"

"I'm saying that instead of wasting my time looking for him, I'm going to find Charlie Spann. What I want you to do is stay put. Don't leave this hotel for any reason."

The murder weapon did not come from the Whitlock estate nor from the Dorrie's. All the guns they owned were antique, behind glass cases, never used.

Selene tried to put it out of her mind, but the vivid likeness of a .22 revolver, old-fashioned, with a long barrel always polished a gleaming blue-black, arose to haunt her. Memories of Charlie and her target practicing with it, rows of bottles along the rock fence of the Spann home; Charlie's intent face, shadows darkening his gray eyes as his finger pressed the trigger sending bottles scattering and shattering.

First she had believed that Wayne was intending to kill her; now she was afraid that Charlie had killed Wayne. Suspicions like some irrational overflow of dam water broke uncontrolled though all resistance.

Sleep was impossible. Could Charlie commit such an act? Charlie's parting words, "I'm going to stop Wayne Dorrie dead in his tracks." Dead! Endless hours of darkness passed as she sat by the window staring at the emptiness of the street below.

By dawn she had come to her senses. The brilliant light that filled the room made her see Charlie again as innocent—as innocent as herself. But how would she be able to prove it? Selene left her room. The lobby was vacant except for a man behind the desk who was sorting papers. Outside the air was crisp. A lull, like in the lobby, hung over the street.

Directly facing her, a man in a business suit waited impatiently for a taxi. Her gaze slid by him to another man. Selene drew in her breath. She had not expected him, after shooting Wayne, to still be watching her!

Selene's first thought was to shrink back into the safety of the hotel and call the sheriff. But with the watcher's uncanny way of showing up and vanishing, he would be gone before the sheriff arrived. And she would lose her opportunity to confront him.

If it had not been for the stable presence of the business man, if she had not been so desperate in her desire to undo the damage she had done to Charlie, she would not have found the nerve to cross the street and move toward him.

As she closed the space between them, he loomed taller, more menacing. His clothes were sweaty, as unkempt as the shaggy beard and hair. The wild glint to his eyes clouded as he watched her approach, became muddy and unreadable.

She was able to control the pitch of her voice, make it even, fearless. "I want to know why you're watching me."

A tense tightening of thick, dry lips was his only response.

"What do you want?" Her voice rose. "Who are you?"

His lips barely moved as he spoke. "Lady, you must have me mixed up with someone else." He turned abruptly and strode off down the street.

Selene hesitated a moment, then followed after him. He swung around the corner out of sight. She half ran trying to catch up, but when she reached the place where he had turned, she found the sidewalk deserted. How could he be out of sight so quickly? Her eyes swept along the buildings, pausing at a restaurant already open for business. Her gaze roamed to the alley. He could be anywhere. It wasn't plausible that she could ever locate him again, or if she could, it would be foolhardy to face him in whatever isolated place he would be hiding.

Selene thought of calling the sheriff, but she knew he would consider this one more story she had made up. She returned to the businessman who still waited for a cab. "The man that was just here. Did you know him?"

"I'm afraid I didn't pay too much attention." He added helpfully, "Is there something wrong?"

"No." Selene could feel questioning eyes follow her as she moved toward her car.

Was the watcher planning to kill her too? Had someone hired him to murder both Wayne and her? That would seem totally without object, for no one person would profit from her death. The Whitlock fortune, falling without contest to her since Wayne died first, would go as her will directed into Whitlock Corporation.

Selene decided to drive by her home first and see if anything was missing. She had expected law officers to still be present at the house, but she had to find her key and unlock the door. Blood on the white carpet beside the couch caused her to recoil. It was inconceivable that no one had attempted to clean it up. Blackness blotted her vision. Trying to prevent herself from fainting, she stopped to lean against the window ledge.

However much she had grown to detest Wayne, she had not wished him dead. She tried not to cry as she tore her gaze from the stains and walked in a random, wooden way from room to room. The most valuable possessions were the swords and guns passed down to her from the Whitlock's war years, priceless relics from Civil War days and before. Selene found the huge glass cases soundly locked. Next she checked the contents of the safe, then through her scattered assortment of jewelry. Nothing missing.

In the front room near where Wayne was killed, her diamond ring lay on the TV. No robber was likely to overlook that. As she stared at the diamond, one fact became certain to her. Wayne's death was not the work of a thief.

Selene felt as if every minute she spent in the house, she was putting her own life in danger, but she had to call Charlie. In the office she dialed his home. Mary, his maid, spoke anxiously, "The sheriff picked him up for questioning." The old lady's voice became tearful. "Mrs. Dorrie, what are we going to do?"

I want you to call Gordon Maxwell, Whitlock's attorney. Tell him to go at once to the sheriff's office."

"Where will you be? Mr. Spann will want to know. The first question he'll ask is, 'Where did Mrs. Dorrie call from?' You're not at home, I know that. No one would be!"

"I'll contact him, Mary. Tell him not to worry about me."

Selene replaced the receiver. She longed to go to the station herself, but she knew it would not help Charlie for her to show up there. She would benefit him more by doing a little investigating on her own. A good place to start was with Wayne's girlfriend, Tammy Dunn.

Selene remembered hearing someone once referring to Tammy as Mrs. Virgil Dunn, but no Virgil Dunn was listed in the phone book, nor were there any Dunns with a south-side-of-town location. An unlisted number perhaps. Surely somewhere among Wayne's papers would be a note. After a long search she found jotted at the top of a notepad: Tam, 5567. Her fingers shook she pressed the numbers. "Hello. I'd like to speak to Mrs. Dunn."

A man's voice told her Tammy was not there.

"I must contact her right away. It's important."

"She left town about three days ago."

"When will she be back?"

"Soon. Maybe today. Who is this?"

"Mrs. Dorrie. I must find her. You see, Tammy often does typing for us. I'll call back."

Selene searched thoroughly through Wayne's belongings, but found nothing. Certainly letters had been exchanged. Somewhere there must be a clue to the existing state of their romance. Maybe she would find some information at the cabin. In late years Wayne had taken it over, was the only one who ever used it.

The isolated retreat was eight miles from town. The Whitlocks had purchased it as a getaway to remove them from the vast responsibilities that marked their lives. Once this lakefront cabin had been a joy to Selene, but after Mother died, Selene had quit thinking of it as a personal haven where Mother had read and Charlie and she had swum, hiked, loafed.

Selene watched alertly in the rear view mirror. For a while a farmer in a pickup truck drove behind her, then an older couple in a black Ford. Nothing to suspect about them. The highway was completely empty when Selene turned. The winding dirt road, water rising very close to it, circled the small lake. The entire east side of it was Whitlock property.

As she neared the cabin, Selene looked for the old boat Charlie and she had so often used for fishing. A memory flashed before her of an unexpected, spring storm and of Charlie, soaked, blinded by rain, vainly paddling. Her eyes fell to the boat now. The wood was beginning to rot. The inside looked water-logged and neglected.

So did the cabin.

The damp spring had caused a thick growth of foliage to encroach close to the building. From the depths of tall oaks and cottonwoods that encircled and secluded it, hung the sharp odor of moist earth and plush vegetation. She paused beside the car and breathed deeply, as if the familiar smell would give her strength.

Tuggings of fear, becoming more persistent, prompted her to stop again. A vision of the watcher, crouched inside, arose, one she tried to battle with logic. Even if the watcher had managed to trail her, it would be impossible for him to arrive here first; just as impossible would be his having a pre-knowledge of the cabin's existence. Only one or two people even knew about it, close friends like Charlie Spann.

Searching for her keys, Selene approached the door. A noise sounded from inside. Her heart sank. Footsteps!

Selene backed away. She raced to the side of the cabin. Pressed against the wall, she waited, holding her breath. The door scraped against the wooden threshold.

She tried to calm herself by thinking of Charlie. The sheriff would not hold him. Charlie's housekeeper must have told him about her call and he could be looking for her here. Almost expecting to see him, she ventured a glance around the corner of the cabin.

Tammy Dunn. She looked like a young girl, almost like a child. She walked out into the yard. What was she doing here?

Selene's thoughts raced. Tammy's husband had said she had left home three days ago. Wayne must have been letting her stay here.

Or had Wayne made promises to Tammy, those shallow, empty promises he made so easily, ones he had no intention of carrying out? A terrible image formed in Selene's mind, of Tammy, infuriated to find out that Wayne was not going to leave the Whitlock fortune for her, pressing the trigger of a .22 revolver again and again. Afterwards Tammy fled to the cabin—they had no doubt made love here—to hide out.

If this had happened, confronting her would do no good. Only in fiction did criminals break down and confess. Moreover, Tammy must still have the gun she had used to shoot Wayne and would doubtlessly be willing to kill again.

Selene watched Tammy look toward Selene's car, look around the yard. Then Tammy called, "Wayne."

Selene left her hiding place. She felt a rush of anger as she came face to face with Tammy Dunn. "This is private property. What are you doing here?"

Short, redish hair hung in a straight, full cut around Tammy's impish, child-like face. Dark pupils in blue eyes enlarged, became huge, frightened. "Wayne," she started. She swallowed, started again, "Wayne told me to..."

Upon the mention of Wayne's name, Selene felt anger drain from her, leave her exhausted, as frightened as Tammy looked. Her voice softened. "You haven't heard about Wayne?"

Tammy's face grew white, magnifying the sprinkle of freckles. "Has something happened to him?"

"I'm afraid so." It was all she could do to go on. "Tammy, Wayne is dead. Someone shot him."

Tammy let out a shriek. She ran back into the cabin. When Selene reached the door, Tammy was seated at the kitchen table, face in hands, thin shoulders rising and falling with each sob.

Poor Tammy. She really did love Wayne. Some of Selene's hardness toward her dissolved. Selene, of all people, could understand the spell Wayne had cast over her. She seemed so very young, so innocent. "Tammy..."

"Don't you know what happened?" Tammy jumped to her feet, shrinking from the horror of her own words. "Virgil killed Wayne! He said he was going to and he did! He said he was going to kill me, too! And he will! Oh, my God! He's crazy!"

"Your husband?" Selene thought of Virgil Dunn's quiet voice on the phone and terror filled her. The watcher was Tammy's husband. After shooting Wayne, he had continued to watch Selene knowing she would lead him to Tammy. How easy Selene had made it for him. She had even placed that stupid call telling him of her immediate intent.

For days from a distance they had observed one another. She thought now of how he had shown up outside Rimrock Hotel. How adept he was at spying, at tracking. Selene moved close to the window, eyes sweeping through wall-like vegetation.

"After Virgil found out about us, Wayne told me to hide out here. He said this was the safest place to be. No one knows about it."

Selene's eyes strained, but saw no sign of Virgil Dunn. Yet she knew he was out there. She could sense his presence just as she had in her home on Marlin Hill. He had managed somehow to follow her here.

"What's wrong?" Tammy's fearful voice demanded. "What do you see?"

"We've got to get out of here. We've no time to waste."

Even as she spoke, her alert eyes caught movement in the trees along the road. Tammy stood close beside her now. Selene was aware of her small frame, shaking. She could hear Tammy's rasping breath, and hear her words, "Oh, no! That's him! He'll kill us both!"

Not even trying to hide, Virgil Dunn broke through the trees into the clearing. There he stopped, watched, listened. His manner was deadly patient, and he stood, slightly hunched, just as he had outside of Selene's house.

He had killed Wayne, bided his time waiting for the right opportunity. He was doing the same with Tammy. Why hadn't it ever crossed her mind that the watcher was Tammy's husband? Why had she made the mistake of aiding him in his ghastly purpose?

He began to approach the door. He had a gun. Selene could tell by the way his hand rested against his belt. They were helpless, totally trapped.

For a moment Selene could not bring herself to move. Then, lunging toward the door, she snapped the bolt. Her action would only postpone the inevitable, but she eagerly snatched at minutes.

Selene dragged the horrified girl away from the window, shaking her slender frame as she spoke, "You must get control of yourself. You're going to have to talk to him. Try to get me some time."

"It's no use!" Tammy screamed. "You don't know him. He's going to kill me."

Selene continued her instructions as if Tammy were rational. "I'm going to climb out the window and find some way to stop him. You must keep talking to him."

Breathlessly she groped through Wayne's tool box in the closet and grabbed a hammer. If only Tammy could keep him distracted....

A pounding started that shook the entrance to the cabin.

"Virgil?" Tammy's small, weak voice sounded like a pathetic, hopeless plea.

"Open the door!"

"You've got to calm down, Virgil. I can't talk to you when you're like this!"

"There's no use talking. There's nothing to say. If you don't open the door, I'll break it down."

"No, Virgil!"

"I killed your boyfriend!"

Tammy moaned.

"No, you killed him! And now you've killed yourself!"

Tammy shrank away from the door

"Slut!" he roared. "I loved you! Slut! Slut!"

Selene finally managed to get the back window open. The last thing she heard before she slipped through it was Tammy's shrieking sob. Feet solidly on the ground, Selene turned, facing the thick trees. In spite of a raging need to hurry, she hesitated. The surrounding trees beckoned to her, a place of safety, of refuge. She could get away. She knew the area so well. The watcher would never be able to track her. She could escape and live.

Selene knew she had no chance at all of overpowering Virgil Dunn. By now he had probably drawn the .22 revolver he had used to kill Wayne. Trying to save Tammy, attempting it, meant certain death.

In the split-seconds that followed, arguments lambasted her, one following another. Tammy, like Wayne, was guilty. She wasn't. Why should she die to save her husband's lover?

And there was Charlie Spann. She would never see him again. He would never know that he was and had always been the most important thing in her life.

The thick trees began to blur. Run, Selene told herself.

But how could she run?

Alertly, eyes clearing, body straightening, Selene forced each step until she had arrived at the corner of the house.

"I'm going to shoot open the lock!" She watched Virgil Dunn step back. The gun, tight in his grasp, angled upward toward the cabin's roof.

Just as he started to level the barrel to the lock, Selene sprang forward. He spotted her, whirled, but before he could aim the gun at her, she struck him with the hammer.

The force of the blow on his temple dazed him. The gun slipped through unclenched fingers. Both hands rose to clutch his head. Blood flowed across one of them, made trails through the scruffy beard, dripped unto his shirt. He swayed.

Why didn't he fall?

Eyes, pain mingled with rage, focused on her. His hands grabbed for her as he staggered forward.

She tried to evade the grasp and reach the gun, but claw-like fingers cut into her neck, her shoulders. They struggled. He was even stronger than she had imagined. She could not break his grip, no matter how frantically she tried. Talon fingers clutched her throat, tightening, tightening, until her gasps for breath were useless.

Virgil's face, the insane eyes, begin to fade and spin. She could no longer see the shaggy beard covered with blood. Where was Tammy? Wasn't she even going to try to stop him?

Selene knew she was still fighting, that her arms and legs were still trying to break free. Intense pain shot from her throat to her chest. Her efforts were hopeless! Tammy had probably climbed out the back window and fled. *It's useless. I'm going to die....*

The killer's grip on her neck slackened at the sound of an approaching car. Then the pressure increased, the pain increased.

Footsteps raced. She couldn't see who was running toward them, but she felt the harsh impact of a body hurled against Virgil's, felt hands being pried from her throat. The hands alone had been holding her up. Freed of them, she was unable to stand. She fell to the ground.

Above her two men, arms locked together, struggled. She wanted to get to her feet, to join again the battle, but her legs and arms refused to obey her. She could barely make out Charlie Spann's lean, strong body, or witness the angry pounding of his fists.

Selene tried again and again to rise and did at last. Breathing was difficult. An agonizing pain filled her lungs. Though half-blinded, she remained on her feet.

Charlie's fist struck Virgil once again. Selene watched in horror as the bearded man staggered away from the blow, took two or three relentless steps toward her, then crumbled at her feet.

Charlie Spann…he must have been searching for her since he was released from the sheriff's office. He drew her into his arms. She could feel the heaving of his chest, the support of his gentle hands. She glimpsed an obscure outline of mussed, blond hair, of sharp features, then she closed her eyes and leaned her head against his shoulder. So comforting. So familiar. Charlie's embrace made the blackness and pain bearable.

~THE END~

About the Authors

Vickie Britton was born in Kansas and now lives in Laramie, Wyoming with her husband Roger and son Ed. She often co-authors with sister Loretta Jackson. They enjoy traveling and their adventures have taken them to Egypt, Europe, and China. Together they have written a mystery series and several mystery-romances. Their work has been produced in paper, audio and electronic format. Vickie's short stories have appeared in *Compassion*, *Minnesota Ink*, and *The Family*.

Loretta Jackson, a former teacher of English and Creative Writing, lives in Junction City, Kansas. She has co-authored with her sister Vickie Britton a number of novels including the Ardis Cole Mystery Series. In the summer, the sisters enjoy traveling in search of intriguing settings for their novels. Loretta's short stories have appeared in the *Kansas Quarterly*, *The Family*, and *Creative Reading*.